I0553315

FÊTE FOR
A KING
by Sam Starbuck

The text of this book is set in Garamond.

This novel is the tenth volume published by
Extribulum Independent Press
extribulum.wordpress.com
Printer's Row, Chicago, IL

Nameless – 2009
Other People Can Smell You – 2009, Revised 2010
Charitable Getting – 2010
Dr. King's Lucky Book – 2011
Trace – 2011
By The Days – 2011
The Dead Isle – 2012
Six Harvests in Lea, Texas – 2020
The Found Fortune Deck – 2022
Fête for a King – 2022

ISBN 979-8-9859604-0-2

This book is the result of an anonymous ask I received in my Tumblr inbox. It is dedicated to that anonymous reader, and more broadly to all the anonymous readers who have come into any of my inboxes to spread joy and inspiration.

PROLOGUE

EDDIE RAMBLER TOOK a bite of the sandwich he'd just been excitedly gesturing with, closed his eyes, groaned, and staggered backwards in pretend shock.

His theatrics didn't bother the octogenarian who had made the sandwich for him in his food truck. Very little had bothered the man, except for when he'd been asked by the episode's director to take off his Red Sox cap because they couldn't have sports logos or unsponsored brand names on the show. There had been a tussle over that which had only been settled when Eddie suggested he turn it around backwards, which had at last led to peace.

Now, watching Eddie pretend to be bowled over by how good his sandwich was, the vendor just grinned and said, "Ya ain't got sammiches like that in California, yeah?"

"Sure ain't," Eddie agreed, pretending to wipe sweat off his forehead. "Hey man, thanks. You know you're the oldest food truck chef I've ever interviewed? What's your secret to a long life?"

"Rye bread," the guy cackled, and Eddie laughed too.

"Thanks for keeping it new even at eighty," Eddie said, clapping him (very gently) on the shoulder. He turned to the camera, gave it a winning smile, and delivered a line he still, somehow, wasn't tired of after five years on air: "And that's…Truly Tasty."

He held the pose until the director gave him a thumbs up, listened for "Wrap on *Truly Tasty*, episode 72!" to reassure him that filming was genuinely over, and then turned back to the sandwich guy again.

"Seriously, this is a great sandwich," he said. "I'll make sure they send you a link when the show goes live."

"You don't issue it on VHS?" the man asked. Eddie paused, horrified, and then relaxed when the man cackled again. "Just pullin' your leg. See you around, huh?"

Eddie nodded and made his way into the crowd of techs, mics, cameras, and all the rest of the small traveling circus required to film an episode of food television, at least the way Eat Network liked to do it. The network was a little old fashioned, but if Eddie wanted to feel cutting-edge he could post to Photogram anytime and keep wooing that under-25 crowd, most of whom (if comments were any indication) were literally learning to cook from Eddie Rambler: celebrity chef, host of *Truly Tasty*, and eater-about-town.

Most of the people running produce stalls at Haymarket, Boston's enormous open-air farmer's market, paid him zero attention other than to look annoyed by all the filming equipment. On the fringes, a few shoppers cast strange looks his way, and a handful of fans were waiting for autographs. Two were even wearing the signature loud floral-patterned shirts he sold on his website, with the linked-T logo on the breast pocket. He stopped only briefly to let hair-and-makeup clean the foundation off his face before he wandered over to the fans.

"Thanks for coming out today, guys," he said, shaking hands and accepting photos, cookbooks, and the odd kitchen implement to sign. "We always appreciate the support."

"Are we gonna be in the show?" one of the younger ones asked. His dad elbowed him gently.

"Tell you what, I'll talk to editing, do my best," Eddie said. "Might not be much of a shot but we'll try, okay?"

"Wicked cool!"

"Sure thing." Eddie gave the kid a fist-bump and winked at his dad. "I'd love to stay but I got a plane to catch. You all keep it new and I'll see you on television, huh?"

He ducked into the tiny trailer that combined equipment storage, lunchroom, and wardrobe into one compact space, grabbing his duffle bag from where he'd stashed it on top of the fridge.

"Is that seriously all you're taking?" one of the PAs asked him, holding out his plane ticket.

"Travel light, kiddo," he said, shouldering the bag. "I've got a phone charger and a credit card, which is more than I had when I started in this business. You need anything else from me? I gotta be at the airport soon but I could shoot some B-roll if we make it quick."

"We'll make do," she replied.

"Great. Hey, pass a note to editing, try and get a few shots with the fans in the loud shirts in the background into this one."

"Got it," she said, noting it down in her phone. It was difficult to get used to people taking him seriously, even when he was being serious. Probably some combination of the floppy bleach-blond hair, chunky sunglasses, and floral shirts; people tended to mistake him for a blue-eyed California himbo without much going on upstairs. Still, that look had gotten him this far, and very few people who met him made the mistake more than once.

"Thanks. And let everyone know I blew town? They've got like eight weeks without my dumb ass looking over their shoulders."

"Quite a vacation," she agreed, grinning. "Where are you going again?"

Eddie hesitated, for once at a loss.

"I'll get back to you on that," he said.

EIGHT WEEKS UNTIL
THE CORONATION OF HIS MAJESTY
KING GREGORY III

THE PALACE OF Askazer-Shivadlakia was enormous in terms of places one might call home, but as castles went it was actually quite small. Gregory's father referred to it as *tasteful*, and most of Gregory's school friends who'd visited said it looked like a setting for a fairy tale, although their tone said the fairy tale was probably a modest one. To Gregory it was simply home, and at the moment he was gazing up at it from the harbor town below, longing to be back there.

Still, occasionally one had to put on the formal dress uniform of the royal family – no medals or sashes, but expensive sober black touched here and there with gold braid – and do a goodwill lap. Especially with the coronation looming. He wanted to make sure that his people understood he was doing his best not to inconvenience them, and that this would all be over in a few months. For them, anyway. For him, it was just beginning.

A local artisan was demonstrating a pattern in the tapestry he was making, which normally Gregory would find interesting, but his mind had begun to drift to everything left to accomplish before the coronation. He glanced up at the palace again, wistfully. Alanna was in the palace, with her reassuring lists and spreadsheets.

The bunting was already out in the town of Fons-Askaz, along with the royal insignia banners and the window decorations featuring Gregory's face. Askazer-Shivadlakia did love its pageantry.

And at least, he thought, as he thanked the artisan and climbed into the car that would take him home, it was one less thing for him to worry about. He relaxed into the seat of the car and took the ride back to the palace to relax and calm his mind.

Alanna was waiting for him at the door, bless her, with a soft sweater for him to change into. Gregory gratefully passed the stiff uniform jacket to his valet and struggled into the sweater as she launched into the report she knew he'd want.

"Flowers are set," she said, gently tugging the collar of the sweater down over his head. He nodded his thanks and pulled it straight. "Just got word this morning."

"Very glad to hear it. Does make me feel as though I'm getting married, however," he replied. "If you tell me I need to pick out a font for the invitations…"

She laughed. "No, I've done that already. And we've made a date for the cleaners to do a deep scrub and airing of all the guest rooms."

"Any word from the tailor? I'd love to have him here sooner rather than later, get the robe fitting out of the way," he said, leading the way down the hall towards his office.

"Working on it. I guess there was some kind of issue getting them out of storage."

"The robes or the tailor?"

"Probably both. He did the fitting for your father's robes too, so he might be immortal."

"Mm. A vampire around the place would certainly add flair," Gregory said, grinning. "And how are the arrangements coming along for father's funeral?"

Alanna actually opened her mouth to answer that, then checked herself and smiled at him.

"Very funny, Your Highness," she said.

"I have to keep you on your toes, Al," he replied.

"His Majesty the king, your father," she drawled, "would like to have dinner with you this evening. He said it was about details for his retirement, but I think he has ulterior motives."

Gregory didn't have a chance to agree with her before he heard his name called, a *basso profundo* shout – "GREGORY!"

He turned towards the source of the roar and saw his father, King Michaelis, at the other end of the hallway, attended by his own crowd of aides and assistants.

"Sometimes it's like he's with me even now," Gregory said to Alanna, who nodded, poker-faced.

"DINNER!" Michaelis called. "TONIGHT!"

"Of course, Father," Gregory called back. Michaelis nodded and stalked onwards, intent on whatever royal business he still had to handle with two months to go until his retirement.

"Oh! And I have great news," Alanna said, checking items off a list on her tablet as they continued. "The chef you asked for? He arrived late last night. He's settling in now, with plenty of time to get the menu set and the catering up and running."

"Ah, the coronation banquet, right," Gregory said, recalling faintly some conversation they'd had about this. "Who'd you get?"

"Eddie Rambler," Alanna said, perplexed. "Like you asked for."

Gregory came to a stop, turning to fully face her. "Eddie... Rambler?"

"The TV chef," Alanna replied. "He hosts *Truly Tasty*?"

"He hosts what," Gregory said flatly.

"I thought you asked..." Alanna began, then hesitated. Gregory had known Alanna since childhood, and the look on her face was very familiar; it was usually a look they gave each other when they'd gotten into some mischief too big to simply scamper their way out of.

"You said...you said you wanted the 'Keep it new' guy, right?" Alanna asked hesitantly.

"I said I wanted someone who would keep things new," Gregory replied, relatively certain that was what he'd said, though his memory of the discussion was cloudy. He'd been distracted by something, probably some request of his father's. "I wanted to show the guests that we're truly a twenty-first century modern monarchy."

"Well...he's definitely modern," Alanna pointed out.

"We hired the host of a TV food show to cater my coronation banquet?" Gregory asked.

Before Alanna could reply, her tablet bleeped; she looked down, equal parts distracted and, he could tell, searching for a distraction.

"He just posted a new Photogram video!" she said brightly, holding the tablet up for him to see, then blinked when she saw Gregory's face. She tried to tuck the tablet away, but he tapped the play button before she could.

Eddie Rambler, six feet of loud blond celebrity chef, had posted a video filmed in the palace kitchen. Gregory's personal palace kitchen, the one that served the royal family directly, not even the larger kitchen that served palace staff and guests.

Gregory tapped the tablet again and raised the volume just in time to hear Rambler say "The Democratic Monarchy of Askazer-Shivad…nokia," followed by an encouraging noise from Simon, the royal family's personal chef. Alanna jerked the tablet away from him and closed the window.

"I was looking for modern like a nice gastropub," Gregory said. "Not like a dive bar." He kept his tone gentle, because he suspected this was as much his fault as hers.

"I am so, so sorry," she said.

"No, it's fine," he replied. "We can explain there was a mistake."

"I thought you'd want a famous chef to do the banquet – "

"These things happen," he told her. "It's a minor speed bump. If that. More like a small pothole."

"Do you want me to tell him today?" she asked. "He just got here."

"No, I should do it," he decided.

"Oh, no, that's not – "

"I'm responsible for the country, and the palace," Gregory told her. "When mistakes are made, regardless of how, I have to fix them gracefully. Anyway, it was just a miscommunication. And I don't punish my staff for honest mistakes."

"Are you sure?" she asked.

"Well, maybe a little," he said, giving her a smile. "Come on, I'm going to make you watch."

She winced, but followed him bravely as he made his way to the palace kitchen.

Eddie set the phone in its little tripod on one of the palace kitchen's stainless-steel prep counters, pressed the record button, and backed up until he was perfectly framed in the phone's selfie-mode reflected footage.

"Well, I told you all I had a surprise for you," he said with a wink. "Guess what? I'm in Europe! I've been hired by the crown prince of…" He faltered, then, sighing. "Ah, man…."

He darted forward to rotate the camera on its tripod; Simon LeFevre, a gray-haired man in pristine chef's whites, had been warned this might happen. He gave the camera a narrow, skeptical look.

"Say it again for me, Chef?" Eddie pleaded.

Simon nodded and poured centuries of French gravitas into his voice as he said, "The Democratic Monarchy of Askazer-Shivadlakia."

Eddie gave him a quick "ok" gesture before turning the camera back on himself.

"I'm gonna get it," he announced. "Here we go. The Democratic Monarchy of Askazer-Shivad..."

Despair rolled briefly through him, even though he knew this would be great content.

"...nokia," he finished, then pressed a hand over his face.

"You're getting closer!" Simon said encouragingly. Like a natural-born star, he leaned in so the phone mic would pick up his voice even though it wasn't recording his face.

"Thanks, Chef," Eddie nodded, letting his hand fall. He put on a fresh smile. "Anyway. I've been invited here by the royal family to cater a coronation banquet. I'll be coming to you live and in living color, only on my Photogram, for the next two months!" he pointed down, to an imaginary logo bug he could add in post. "So if you want all the news, remember to subscribe!"

Simon looked at him like Eddie's ancestors were ashamed of him, but Eddie made *sacrifices* for his followers.

"It's crazy here," he continued. "I'm staying in a genuine palace and everything! I promise lots of content, some tours if I can sneak past the palace guard, plenty of quick cooking lessons, and hopefully a few selfies with the royals. Okay, that's all for now – peace out and you know I mean it when I say: keep it new!"

He shot the camera the peace sign, then hurried forward to end the recording. Simon went back to the stove, shaking his head, but Eddie knew he'd charmed the reserved Frenchman. He picked up his phone and made a few hasty adjustments to the video before slamming that post button with a paragraph's worth of hashtags.

"I really wanted to get that right," he said as he worked. "Help me out? Askazer..."

"Shivadlakia," Simon repeated.

"Shivadlakia," Eddie managed.

"It takes time to learn to let it roll off the tongue," Simon said. "The important thing is to try."

"Well, trying's all I have," Eddie said, settling himself on a stool near the prep table. "You sure you don't mind me in your kitchen?"

"No, I have seen your show," Simon said. "I know you are a true chef in a carnival barker costume."

Eddie clutched his chest, but Simon was unperturbed by his suffering. A timer went off on Eddie's phone, and he hurried to one of the four nearby ovens, pulling out the cast-iron pot he'd had in there.

"Here we go," he said, removing the lid and inhaling the fragrant steam. Simon peered into it, interested. "Looks great. You want a sample? Hey, when do you think I'll get to meet the prince?"

Simon looked past him, towards the doorway of the kitchen.

"Very soon," he murmured, and Eddie turned.

Crown Prince Gregory ben Michaelis, soon to be King Gregory III of This Place He Was Definitely Going To Memorize The Name Of Soon, stood in the doorway. Eddie had done at least a little research, but even if he hadn't, Gregory's face was everywhere. There were even posters in the train station announcing his coronation and welcoming tourists and diplomats who were going to be attending. Still, it took a few seconds for it to sink in. This was a royal prince, after all, and he was also insanely hot.

The posters and photographs didn't do justice to the deep olive of his skin or the short-cropped dark curly hair above equally dark eyes; in the pictures he was wearing a high-collared, gold-edged dress jacket, but the real prince was wearing a burgundy sweater with a simple diamond pattern across his shoulders, as well as a somewhat imposing expression. Behind him, a slight young woman with long brown hair, a sweet face, and a tablet clutched in one hand looked extremely alarmed.

"Prince Gregory," Eddie heard Simon say. "May I introduce Chef Edward Rambler. Chef, this is His Highness, Crown Prince Gregory."

"Whoa," Eddie said, and then screamed, briefly, internally. He'd done enough panicking on enough national broadcasts to keep from doing it externally, at least.

"Beg pardon?" the prince asked, blinking.

Eddie decided to lean into his initial reaction. "Whoa! Wow, here you are! Your Highness! It's such a pleasure. Do I bow, or do I shake hands?"

"Either is acceptable," Simon told him, clearly teasing, at the same time the prince said, "Ah yes, Mr. Rambler. I – "

"Oh, call me Eddie," Eddie said, deciding on the handshake and reaching out. Prince Gregory took his hand automatically; he had a firm handshake even when surprised. Nice hands, too. Warm. Eddie ignored that and leaned around the prince, because he'd just realized who the alarmed woman was.

"Alanna, right?" he asked, shooting her finger-guns because the prince was in the way of a second handshake.

She nodded, and Eddie turned back to the prince. "This lady is great! She hired me and really got me set up. I'm super excited to be here to help out with the coronation. It's a new one for me."

"Ah, yes, about that," the prince said, and Eddie knew an opening for a pitch when he saw one. He held up a hand.

"Don't say another word yet," he warned. "I know you probably have a vision for your coronation banquet, but I want to rock your world for a second before we dish." The prince started to say something, but Eddie was already heading for the pot he'd just taken from the oven, and he'd sold enough hard ideas to enough rich show-business types to know that the key was continually talking until they broke down.

"So a banquet is a big deal, but you hired me, right?" he asked, rummaging in a drawer for a tasting spoon. Simon handed him one. "Thanks, Chef. So I know you want to keep it new, and I figure maybe a little relaxed. It's a formal occasion but we can set a real easygoing tone with the food, make sure it's comfortable as well as high-brow. The hard part's over by the time you get to the feast, right? So I have a ton of ideas but just consider this first: hot sandwich bar."

He scooped up a mini-meatball, made sure it had plenty of sauce on it, and turned to the prince, who said, "I really need to – "

"Taste this, I know!" Eddie replied. "It smells amazing, but trust me, there's truth in this advertising."

"You see – " the prince tried again, but Eddie held the spoon in front of his face.

"Here, taste," he commanded. It was, actually, a little gratifying that even a prince couldn't disobey the command to try some of Eddie's food. He took the spoon from Eddie's hand and sampled the mini-meatball with genuine consideration. Simon was already offering another one to Alanna on a toast point.

"Tarragon mini-meatballs in red pepper marinara," Eddie announced. "You get a big pan of these and you stuff 'em in an olive oil roll with some fresh basil or rosemary…"

The prince had finished chewing; Alanna was watching him, her mouth still full, and it only then dawned on Eddie that there might be a subtext to the conversation that he wasn't privy to.

"You made this, just now?" the prince asked, swallowing.

"Well, I improvised with what Simon had lying around," Eddie admitted. "If you don't like the flavor profile we could go with a traditional marinara, maybe a little more garlic in the *meats'a'ball*…"

He put a fake-Italian accent on the last word, trying to anchor them firmly in the lighthearted world he'd been pitching, but all Prince Gregory said was, "This is your concept for the banquet?"

"Well, one idea, sure," Eddie ventured. "Easy to prepare, easy to serve, keeps the line moving. Not just these, obviously. You get five or six different hot dishes – meatballs, some spicy chicken, sausage, sweet potato curry or fried butternut squash for a vegetarian option – and you got some guys dishing the hots into the breads. Add a condiment bar, you're good to go. Passed apps beforehand, plenty 'a side dishes. Simon says he'll do the cake, which is great, because I am many things but I am not a pastry chef."

He watched the prince carefully, but the man had a pretty good poker face. Now was perhaps the time to let things simmer, to let him consider; Eddie glanced at Alanna, who had been both kind and fun to talk to when setting all this up, but she was still eyeballing her boss.

"Well," Prince Gregory said finally, "It's a little informal for what I had in mind, but I'll consider it as an option."

"Red sauce," Eddie replied. "Nobody resists the red sauce. Up top!"

He held up his hand for a high-five, but he had definitely misjudged something about the situation. The prince just stared at him. Eddie shot a pleading look at Alanna, and after a split second she leaned around the prince and finished the high-five. Well, he at least had one ally on the royal side.

"Simon," the prince said, turning to the other chef. "Include these with dinner tonight, if you would. Father will want to try them. Service as Mr. Rambler – "

"Eddie," Eddie said. "Or Dude," he added jokingly.

It backfired immediately. "Service as Mr....Dude recommends," the prince finished. "I'd like to see a range of your 'hot sandwich' options, but I'll want some menus for a multi-course sit-down dinner as well, and perhaps a few other concepts as they come to you. Speak to Alanna tomorrow morning about a meeting, when you're ready, to go over your ideas."

"You got it," Eddie answered, hiding most of his glee and all of his amusement. The prince, without another word, turned and left the kitchen, Alanna trailing behind him with a little wave goodbye.

Eddie glanced at Simon and saw Simon was already looking sidelong at him. Eddie broke first; Simon didn't exactly crack up laughing, but once Eddie started to laugh he deigned to give him a good-natured chuckle.

"Mr. Dude," Eddie hooted. "Oh man. What a stuffed shirt."

"He's a good man at heart," Simon replied, shaking his head. "I've known him from a child. He'll govern well."

"Hope so for your sake," Eddie said. "Anyway, doesn't matter. He liked the meatballs and I can work with the rest. I just gotta un-stuffify him a little."

"I wish you luck in your quest," Simon told him, and went back to prepping for dinner.

Gregory didn't stop walking until he was in his office, down the hall from the kitchen. It was the place he was most at home, at least nowadays. In the middle of the room, with its bookshelves and worktable, wide bay windows and prized antique telescope, he felt like he could, in fact, rule wisely. At the moment he felt mostly taken aback; he turned to face Alanna, not sure what to say.

"So," Alanna said finally, after a few seconds of silence. "Good job firing him back there."

"I didn't know he could actually cook," Gregory said, because it was all he could think about. The little spoonful of food, a simple meatball in piping hot sauce, had shocked him into silence. Simon was a good chef and had taught Gregory to appreciate good food, and apparently Rambler knew a thing or two about good food too.

He also hadn't thought the man would be quite so good-looking in person. On the television, on the rare occasions Gregory had seen it in passing, he always looked sort of…

Well, trashy. Might as well admit to his own snobbery. In person, moving, speaking excitedly, he was a very good looking man. Tall, with dark gold hair bleached white at the tips and deep blue eyes, he had a compellingly mobile face. And that ridiculous flowery shirt didn't hide the fact that the man was built like a…like a Viking, or a tree. A Viking tree, perhaps. Solid enough to climb.

"I didn't know he could cook like that," Alanna admitted.

"It was really good!" Gregory exploded.

"I know!" Alanna replied, equally surprised and excited.

"Is all his food that good?"

"I hope so!"

"He just made that up out of whatever was lying around…" Gregory circled his desk, dropping into his chair. "Alanna, not firing him would uncomplicate both our lives."

"Mine more so than yours, but yes," she said.

"And he can cook."

"He can *cook*," she agreed. Gregory understood the distinction. He could still taste the faint bite of sweet pepper in the sauce.

"Okay. So we have a chef. That's good! We'll just find a way to tame his…natural exuberance in front of my father. And maybe me," he added ruefully. Alanna carefully wasn't smiling. Gregory pointed at her. "In the meantime, you're on high-five duty. In fact, that's now a permanent part of your job. I'm appointing you to high-five anyone who wants me to high-five them."

That did break out one of her better smiles, the one that dimpled her cheeks. He saw it less now, as her boss, than he had when they were children and she was his friend. She still was his friend, it was just… boundaries were being renegotiated in light of his coronation.

"You're lucky you're pretty," she said. "I have a few things to deal with. Do you want me to set you an alarm for dinner with His Majesty?"

"No, I've got it covered," he said, and she turned to go. "Don't wear yourself out," he added, genuinely concerned.

"I'm fine. Save me a meats'a'ball!" she called as she left.

The palace had a formal dining room of course, for state dinners and feasts and the various diplomatic parties Michaelis had thrown and Gregory would be expected to. It was a big, echoing room with unfortunate baroque decor that Gregory would like to streamline, but the historians would clutch their pearls. The family dining room, where the royal family ate most of their meals, was smaller and more modern, not subject to the same attempt at awe as most of the palace. Gregory arrived just as the hot dishes were being set on the table, and saw a rustic bowl of Eddie Rambler's meatballs placed at his father's elbow, along with a plate of crusty bread.

"Quiet day?" he asked Michaelis, helping himself to a cup of stew while his father dished up some of the meatballs.

"For the most part. Every day I do a little less," his father replied. "Bread?"

"Please, and I'll take those when you're done, too," Gregory replied. Michaelis passed over the bread, then took the stew in exchange for the meatballs. "Well, that's the point of the handover, so that the chaos is out of the way before the coronation."

"Having gone through my own, I can tell you, you're very optimistic about how well these things work," Michaelis replied.

"You know me, Crown Prince Optimism," Gregory said. "I'm sure there'll be wrinkles, but it's not like you're leaving for an eight-month cruise like Grandfather did when you were crowned."

"Never forgave him for that."

"You seemed to recover," Gregory pointed out, amused. "Something in particular you wanted to discuss?"

"I can't enjoy dinner with my only son and heir?"

Gregory grinned at him. "You can, but you sounded like you had something on your mind earlier."

"Well, sort of. I received some comments about your impending reign today."

Gregory sat up straighter, perturbed. If his father's aides were questioning his competency, or worse, some of the parliament members –

"Don't look so distraught, it's nothing to do with your qualifications," Michaelis said soothingly. "Anyway, I'd fight that battle for you if they questioned them. I've taught you all I know about statecraft and diplomacy. And I think some of those fancy schools I sent you to taught you something about economics."

"I didn't mail-order the MBA," Gregory agreed.

"I hope not. If you did, I overpaid. No, I think you're ready to be king and most people agree with me. And I'm very proud of that," Michaelis added, giving him a meaningful look.

Gregory narrowed his eyes. "And thank you."

Michaelis set down his spoon. "But I think once the coronation is over, it's time to seriously consider finding a partner."

Ah. Back to that, then.

He supposed it was good of Dad to face the issue head-on, at least. A lot of royals would either ignore an inconveniently gay son or try to evangelize him back to heterosexuality. Michaelis had always been good about not doing that, and once he'd gotten past the initial surprise, he'd been supportive. Still, it didn't stop him from insisting on a semi-annual discussion of Gregory's lack of a husband.

"Dad," he began warily, and Michaelis winced, cutting him off.

"I know, I know you don't want to rush things, but this is important. You need someone who can make sure your plans go forward if you get sick – or, Heaven forbid, you die."

"This is great dinner conversation."

"Would you prefer it be breakfast conversation?" Michaelis asked, which was an annoyingly good point. "You need someone to be able to step in at a moment's notice, someone who carries the authority of the king without needing all the paperwork to back them up. It's not just that, either. The people should see that you have a…a backup plan. It's for the stability of the kingdom as much as anything else."

"I just don't think the backup plan has to be a spouse," Gregory said.

"Yes, I heard you the last time someone brought this up. You can think all you want, Gregory, but that won't turn the tide of public opinion. You need a visible, present, and appropriate helpmeet and workmate."

"I have Alanna."

"And if you married Alanna, cousins or not, there would be great celebration in the country," Michaelis said. "But as it stands now she won't be your assistant forever. And she deserves someone who could give her more than a sham marriage. You aren't going to marry Alanna."

"No," Gregory admitted.

"Good," Michaelis said, surprising him. He blinked across the dinner table at his father.

"Good?"

"See, here's the part I don't think you ever hear when this comes up," Michaelis said, leaning forward a little. "You need a companion too, son. It's hard going this alone. You need someone you can vent to at the end of the day – someone who looks after you and lets you look after them. You need a refuge from the throne. Like your mother was for me."

"Doubly unfair to Alanna, then. She wouldn't get much in return and she wouldn't even get paid for it anymore," Gregory said, trying to lighten the moment. His mother Miranda's death was still a tender topic years later, but if his father was going to pitch it this way, he had to ask. "Who's been there for you since Mom died?"

"Never mind that. We're talking about you, not me," Michaelis said shortly, which was precisely the kind of non-answer he always gave when Gregory brought her up. "Look, we are very traditional in some ways but you know nobody here would care if you had a king consort instead of a queen, and there are options for heirs. You just have to have *someone*."

"King consort," Gregory snorted.

"Fine, give him whatever title you like."

"Duke of Buckingham."

"Eh what?" Michaelis asked, looking puzzled.

"Sorry. Dumb joke," Gregory said. "James the First of England had a boyfriend. He made him Duke of Buckingham."

"Well, then make him a duke, it doesn't matter," Michaelis said, waving it away with typical Shivadh arrogance, as if the monarchy of England was a minor concern next to the throne of Askazer-

Shivadlakia. "The point is, whoever or whatever he is, he'll need to be brought up to speed on royal etiquette, start learning to step in for you if he has to. He'll have to have all kinds of PR briefings."

"You're not really selling me on this," Gregory pointed out. His father, halfway through a bite of meatball, didn't reply. "There's not a lot of spare time. You know better than anyone that running the country takes a lot of work."

"And you know better than anyone that one has to make time for one's family," Michaelis said, and then delivered the killing blow. "If you don't, I'll do it for you."

Gregory set his silverware down. "No."

"I could hold a ball," Michaelis threatened.

"Dad, no – "

"Every eligible bachelor in the country," Michaelis said with relish. "I'll import a few. A foreign spouse is always good for diplomatic relations. Maybe one or two millionaires from America."

"You can't," Gregory protested, even though he knew his father was joking.

Probably. Mostly.

"There will be waltzing," Michaelis said darkly.

"You wouldn't dare."

"Then you've got to do it yourself," Michaelis retorted. Gregory sighed. "At least think about it, all right? Get Alanna to help, she knows all your exes, and she probably has better taste than you do."

"Now that's just mean."

"It's you, or Alanna, or the Ball," Michaelis said, spooning one of the meatballs onto a crust of bread and popping it in his mouth as if that decided things.

"Fine," Gregory replied, more than ready to change the subject. "I'll talk to her. What do you think of those meatballs, by the way?"

Michaelis swallowed thoughtfully. "Pretty good. I was just thinking I should ask Simon to put them on the regular rotation. A bit different from his usual."

"The new chef made them, the one Alanna hired to do the coronation banquet," Gregory said.

"Well, he seems talented. Although I don't know about meatballs in red sauce for a coronation."

"I've asked him for some other ideas. I think he has plenty."

"I look forward to hearing more," Michaelis said. "All right, let's lay business to rest. I've been thinking of overseeing some upgrades to the fishing lodge…"

In the groves of the palace grounds the next morning, the dew was drying and the sun was barely peeking over the mountains. Birds were bathing or hunting breakfast, the sky overhead was a deep cloudless blue, and the light was at the perfect angle for filming.

"Good morning to everyone who's keeping it new on Photogram!" Eddie said. "It's a beautiful day. I've had a good breakfast – thank you Simon – and I'm escaping the palace early today."

He started to walk, keeping the selfie stick as stable as he could, trying to capture as much of the natural beauty behind him as possible. "I think the first thing a good chef in a strange new country should do is get out and socialize. Meet the people, learn about what they're eating, start tracing that path from farm to table, you know? So here I go!"

He twisted to show them the road down to the village, walking backwards briefly, the quaint glow of lit houses visible behind him.

"I'm going to learn everything there is to know about…" he paused dramatically and then squinted down at his hand, "Askazer-Shivadlakia."

He held up his hand to the camera, grinning, showing the words written on it. "Nailed it. Anyway, I'm going to be way too busy eating everything and meeting everyone to take video myself, but keep your eyes peeled for photos! I'm sure it'll be Truly Tasty."

He finished with a wave at the camera, ended the recording, and uploaded it without even any editing. Practically rustic, and very satisfying. With a clean heart and a hunger to learn, he picked up his pace heading into town.

Gregory ben Michaelis hadn't become crown prince of a small country by sleeping in, any more than Eddie Rambler had become a television star that way. Some of his staff didn't love morning meetings, so he made concessions and never started one before 8:30. Still, by the time the daily briefing rolled around, he was more than ready with marching orders for the day, taking in reports and handing out assignments.

He was just finishing up when the beeping began.

"Lastly," he said, "I know it feels like this is some kind of strange summer break before school starts again, but there are things we just can't start work on until after the coronation."

Alanna's phone beeped, but she ignored it, so he did as well. "This is why it's so important that after the coronation, we be ready to hit the ground running," he continued. "Do what you can now and keep the first month of the new reign – "

Her phone beeped again. Gregory shot her a questioning look, but she shook her head, not looking at it, mouthing, "Sorry."

"Keep the first month of the new reign free," he said. "I mean entirely free. No concert tickets, no hot dates."

The staff laughed, which almost covered the sound of a third beep. Alanna looked down at her phone, finally silencing it, then frowned.

"I promise I'll make it up to you once we're on stable ground," Gregory finished. "Okay. Most of you, your suffering is over for the day. Those with morning meetings with me, get yourself some food, give the kitchen your lunch orders, and come back to settle in."

They filed out, chatting amongst themselves, and Gregory caught Alanna by the elbow before she could leave.

"Even for you that was a lot of texts," he said, smiling to show he wasn't annoyed. "New boyfriend being clingy, or should I worry for the state of my country?"

She gaped at him. "Uh…it's the country, actually."

A brief shot of adrenaline ran through him; his father had handled various crises over the years, and this might be his first.

"What's wrong?" he asked. "Why didn't you interrupt the meeting if it was serious? Has something – "

"No, sorry, it's not…" She rested her hand over his, reassuring. "There's no emergency, exactly. They were status updates from the palace communications office, I just need to find out what's going on. Traffic to the national website is spiking."

"The national website? Like – are we being *hacked?*" he asked in disbelief.

"Not the government intranet. The tourism site," she said, and then did a double take. "Did you just ask if we're being hacked?"

"We might be! Why is the tourist website getting traffic, are we in the news?"

"I'm not sure…" Alanna brushed past him to the small television mounted in one of the bookshelves. "I asked them to find out how people are finding us, what they're searching to get there…"

Her phone beeped again as she was turning on the television, and she blinked at it. "Oh. Ah."

"Oh, ah?" Gregory echoed.

"Well, the good news is, I don't think anything bad has happened," Alanna said.

"What's the bad news?"

She gestured with her phone at the television.

"…nation of Askazer-Shivadlakia is trending this morning after a series of Photogram posts from celebrity chef and influencer Eddie Rambler," a news anchor said, as an image of Rambler appeared next to her.

"Eddie Rambler crashed our website," Alanna said, her voice rising in suppressed amusement.

"Rambler has been hired by Crown Prince Gregory ben Michaelis to cater his coronation banquet," the anchor continued, and then she smiled, and Gregory had a great foreboding. "What everyone seems to want to know this morning, though, is whether Prince Gregory is looking for a queen."

Gregory's official royal portrait, which they had admittedly posted as part of the press packet on the tourism website, replaced Rambler's. Alanna giggled softly as Gregory hit mute.

"He posted a video to Photogram this morning and he's been putting up photos ever since," she said.

"Find him and calm him the hell down," Gregory said.

"I have to say," Alanna continued, ignoring him and scrolling Photogram on her phone, "he's doing a great job of showing off the country. Great PR, if you ask me."

"I don't need good PR, Alanna! I need to get through my first few months as king without the entire world staring at us."

That was a good point he hadn't even thought he was making until he made it, and it snapped Alanna out of her amusement.

"I'll put someone on it," she agreed. "Look, this is why you hired a social media manager for the palace. It'll be fine. Katie's probably feeling very smug."

"Katie in Communications?" Gregory asked, sidetracked.

"She's been telling us to bolster our site infrastructure since the coronation was announced and she got louder about it once she heard a famous chef was coming to cater for us."

"Ah, the joys of I-told-you-so," Gregory nodded. "Look, don't – don't yell at Rambler or anything," he added, because Rambler probably hadn't done it intentionally. Photogram had a way of just…getting out of hand. At least he assumed; he didn't have one personally, but it seemed like Alanna was always telling him about some drama the other noble cousins were getting into on the app. "Don't make him take down the videos, just tell him to tone it down."

"Of course," Alanna said. "Let me handle it, you have meetings all morning."

"I very much do," Gregory sighed. "Okay. Budgets."

"Top left drawer, and in the Finance folder on the shared drive."

"Right. I'll take it from here, you deal with the website situation."

"Always a pleasure, Your Highness," she said.

Once she was gone, he turned the television off entirely, muttering *looking for a queen* dismissively under his breath. That was the last joke he needed anyone to make right now, including himself, but it was a little bit funny, he supposed. He wondered if he should get a Photogram of his own, just for spin control, or to see what Rambler had actually said about the country. Or about him.

Then his staff started trickling back in, at least the ones he needed to meet with, and the idea was shuffled to the back of his mind to make way for more important affairs of state.

Eddie was in a bakery in town, elbows-deep in bread dough and loving life, when the Palace caught up with him. He didn't even know they'd been chasing, but he supposed he should have expected it.

"Mr. Rambler?" came a voice, and Eddie began extracting himself from the dough, while the baker who had been graciously teaching him how to make Askazer twist-bread looked on in amusement. "Eddie?"

"The invitation to call me Dude extended to you, light of the palace," Eddie replied, finally getting free and turning around to face her. The baker's teenaged daughter, who was filming him with her phone, hastily ended the video when she saw who it was. "Did I miss an appointment?"

"You crashed the internet," Alanna said, a hint of a smile twitching around her lips.

"I hate it when I do that," Eddie said to Baker Junior, who giggled at him. "Hey, shoot me that video, would you? Have you got a Photogram?" At her nod, he added, "Then you edit and post it, tag me, and I'll link to yours. We'll get you to influencer in no time. Okay," he continued, rubbing his hands together to clean them of dough and turning back to Alanna. "What'd I do again, now?"

"You namedropped the country on your social media," Alanna continued. "It brought down our tourism website."

"Oh, snap. I didn't even think about that. Is it causing a lot of problems?" Eddie asked, frowning. "Are people like trolling the prince or something?"

"No, but it's giving Communications a headache," she said. "The palace would just like you to tone down the media blitz a little."

"Oh sure, I can pull back on posting to a couple of times a day, at least when it comes to PR stuff. I was just having a great time, there's so much good food here. If I'd known Aska…"

He looked imploringly at her.

"No, you have to learn to say it," she said, hands on hips.

"She's onto me," Eddie said to the baker. "Aska…zer…Shivad… lakios."

"So, so close," she replied, finally grinning.

"If I'd known *your country* had food this good I would have been here years ago. I'm about to be the guy who discovered Askazer twist-bread and brought it to the masses."

"The masses here have had it for about five hundred years," Alanna replied.

"Touché."

"Look, I'm really sorry," she continued, subtly leading him out of the bakery's kitchen. "Truth is, the prince doesn't need more eyeballs on him right now."

"I mean, he's throwing a coronation."

"That's why," she said. "It's not that I want you to stop talking, because we could use the tourism. We just weren't ready for…you."

"I'm not trying to condescend here, but I just obliterated your tourism website, so I need to ask: do you actually have a Communications office?" he said. There was a dark car decorated with the seal of the government parked nearby; it was clearly where she was headed, but he hadn't quite finished his tour yet.

"We do – "

"Oh, sweet, then no problem. I'll just coordinate with them. I do it all the time when I do state tours. I'll have my guy back in the US send me the standard packet, we can make up a strategy," he said brightly. "I love a strategy."

"You do," she repeated, clearly disbelieving, as someone got out of the car and held the door for them.

"I do, I live for that stuff. Okay, like, this is fine," he said, waving to the car, "But I need five minutes. It's for salami. Can I have five minutes for salami?"

He could see Alanna weighing whether this would actually be five minutes or closer to fifty; he squeezed his thumb and forefinger together, pleadingly.

"It's going to look really bad if I have Security pull you out of a salumeria," she told him.

"Yes!" he pumped his fist and raced for the storefront he'd seen earlier, with cured meats in the window. He burst inside and hustled up to the bemused clerk behind the counter.

"I have this much money and I want one of everything," he said, holding up a bill he'd changed from American money earlier.

"Not enough," the man shook his head, but he was already pulling various paper-wrapped sausages together. "I'll give you the tourist package plus fish salami."

"Fish salami," Eddie breathed, eyes widening. "That sounds terrible."

The man grinned. "It is. Punishment for being pushy."

"I'll come back and behave better, I promise," Eddie said, passing the cash across and getting a bundle of anonymous tubes in return. "Which one's the fish?"

"That's for you to discover," the man told him.

Back outside, Alanna was looking at her phone. As he skidded to a stop in front of her, she held it up, showing a timer at the 4:30 mark.

"See, thirty seconds to spare," he said as he climbed into the car, stuffing salami into an already very full messenger bag. Alanna, sliding in after him, offered her purse. He put what he hoped wasn't the fish salami into it. "There's more where that came from."

"You'd be surprised how many men tell me that," she informed him gravely.

"I like you more every hour, Alanna."

"Probably for the best, because I'm here mainly to spoil everyone's fun," she told him. "Driver, to the palace, please."

"I thought that was Prince Gregory's job, spoiling the fun."

"Unkind." She swatted him gently on the arm. "His Highness has a lot on his mind right now."

"And it's your job to smooth the way, eh?" he asked.

"I do what I can. I'm very good at it and I enjoy it, so it's not usually as annoying as I pretend," she said with a grin.

"I think you and I are gonna get along just fine," Eddie replied. "You set me up with your people and I'll text my PR folks, and in the meantime we'll pretend to be a power couple off to take over Monaco, how's that sound?"

"We did once try to invade Monaco, around the 16th century or so," Alanna said.

"Imagine what might have been," Eddie told her solemnly.

Askazer-Shivadlakia was not a large country, or politically important, or particularly wealthy. Traditionally, ruling it was tedious, but rarely a struggle; a good job for a man who liked math and thought diplomacy was exciting. Gregory did sometimes wonder if earlier kings got as stressed out by olive crop yields as he did, and if they'd felt as much like they were drowning when they came up on the coronation.

From where he sat, on the bench under the big bay window of his office on the palace's ground floor, he could see a couple of the old kings – two were in portraits in his office, and one (so it was rumored) was buried in the ornamental garden just past the road leading up to the palace entrance. The sun was setting over the grounds, turning the garden golden and the road into a deep black streak among the grassy hills. He'd meant to move away from his desk for a few minutes to enjoy his dinner, but he'd only picked at the meal, and now he was lost in contemplation of the sunset.

There was a smart double-rap on the door frame, Alanna's efficient knock. From the doorway, she said, "Penny for your thoughts."

He sighed, not looking around. "Shivadh currency is pretty strong right now. You could get a lot more and better thoughts for a penny in France."

"I like the personal touch. Hand-crafted by a traditionalist," she replied. He turned to shoot her the best smile he could manage. "I mean it, Greg. Anything I can help with?"

"No, not yet," he said, turning back to the landscape. "Just ticking off a few things on the to-do list. Stuff I've been avoiding for a week."

"Like what?"

He shrugged. "You ever stop and look at something you're doing and think maybe you bit off more than you can chew?"

"Yeah, the first six months I worked for you," Alanna replied, coming to sit on the other end of the bench, more or less forcing the conversation. It was something he appreciated about her; she knew when to push.

"I wasn't that bad," Gregory protested. "Besides, you knew what you were getting into."

"Even for you it was a lot," she told him.

"It wasn't."

"You were named crown prince and your first diplomatic act afterward was to adopt a puffin while you were on vacation in Iceland."

"I rescued the puffin," he retorted, still annoyed that she was bringing up the puffin a year later. "And I gave it back. You don't give things back if you adopt them."

Alanna smiled. She also knew that needling him about the puffin might take him out of himself a little. He rolled his eyes at her.

"So, what puffin is worrying you this time?" she asked. "Even if I can't help as your staff, I can help as your friend."

"It's probably more a staff problem," he said. "Dad's brought up some deficiencies in my palace management."

Alanna's brow furrowed as she frowned. "Like what?"

"I think I need to put a meeting on my calendar," he said. "Make it two – no, three months from now. When we're well clear of the dust of the coronation."

"Okay," she agreed, opening the case on her tablet. "Who's attending?"

"You, me, head of Communications for a start," he said. "Head of our tourism office, too. And add my father but make his invite optional."

"Sure," she replied, fingers dancing over the screen. "What do I call it?"

"Initial planning meeting, royal wedding," he said.

"Getting married?" Alanna asked, laughing. When she saw his expression, the laughter stopped abruptly. "I mean, really? Do...do I know him?"

"Not yet. Well, probably not," Gregory replied. "I need you to help me find him. It's a planning meeting to manage finding me a spouse. Come prepared to brainstorm."

"If you want me to set you up – "

"No, I don't want to rope romance into this," he said. "I want to find someone appropriate. I need a king consort, not a boyfriend. Diplomatic, preferably royalty from somewhere nearby or with sufficient wealth that he knows what he's getting into. Potentially open-minded on the subject of adopting children and having extramarital affairs."

Alanna, quietly, closed her tablet case again.

"Greg," she said.

"I told you this was a staff thing, not a friend thing."

"You cannot meeting-minutes yourself a husband," she said.

"I'm sure it's been done. Probably by kings before me," he pointed out.

"Love isn't a function of government!"

"I'm not looking for love, Al. I'm too busy for that. But Dad's not wrong that I need a partner, and the sooner the better. If we find someone with a reasonably even temper and decent ego we can make it work. Actually, a narcissist might be just the thing," he said thoughtfully.

"Might as well just marry me," she said.

"That's what Dad said. I would, but it'd hardly be fair to you. Anyway, I'm already out; people would know it was a sham if I did that. And you deserve a paycheck for what you put up with."

"But your husband doesn't?"

"It's not like being king consort doesn't have perks. And if I like the look of him and he doesn't mind me, we could make something work. I know it's a tall order but there can't be that big a shortage of sensible, good-looking gay men in Europe."

"There's a shortage of that in this room," Alanna drawled.

"Ouch!"

"I just mean you're not being sensible. But you are being…royal," Alanna sighed. "I don't suppose Jerry – "

"Jerry's my cousin," Gregory said.

"So am I!"

"Yeah, but you're disqualified for other reasons. Anyway, Jerry's also straight. And a buffoon."

"People like a buffoon. Fine, not Jerry," Alanna said. "I'll start a list, but I'm doing this under protest."

"If you think about it, a husband-search is probably the most royal thing I've done," Gregory said, as she opened the tablet again.

"Royal pain in my ass," Alanna retorted. "Invite sent, but we will be circling back on this."

"You and my father both. Your country thanks you for your service."

"Hm." She stood up, tucking the tablet under one arm. "Try to get to bed before midnight, huh? The spreadsheets will wait a day."

"That's a lie, but I'll do my best."

He let her kiss him on the forehead, then turned back to the window as she left.

SEVEN WEEKS UNTIL
THE CORONATION OF HIS MAJESTY
KING GREGORY III

AFTER DRAGGING THE entire internet to their doorstep, where Askazer-Shivadlakia became a meme for about 29 hours, Eddie Rambler laid low. At least that was what Gregory assumed he was doing. He didn't see him much around the palace, and while Rambler didn't stop posting completely, he did seem to be working well with palace communications about when and where to share his glamorous life in a small European kingdom. Gregory asked Alanna for a daily update on the Photogram situation, but after two days of that Alanna took his phone away and maliciously installed Photogram on it so that he had to check it himself. He considered using his new account to become an influencer, just to annoy her, but that would have been funnier when they were kids.

He was just finishing up for the day, about to check Photogram as a break from paperwork, when he looked up from his desk and caught sight of the chef through his window.

At first he didn't realize who it was; the sun was down and the figure on the road wasn't much more than a vaguely two-legged shape against the last red of sunset, with a weird bulge on one side and a single, strange antenna. He moved to the window, open to let in the summer air, and confirmed to himself that it was Rambler. The bulge was a bag slung over one shoulder, and the antenna resolved itself into an archery bow.

Before he could withdraw, satisfied, Rambler saw him and lifted his bow in greeting, cutting across the grass to the window instead of following the road.

"Evening, Your Highness," Rambler said, coming to rest his arms on the ledge of the window, just below chest-height. "Working late?"

"Good evening, Mr. Rambler," Gregory said, feeling strangely formal and awkward, standing above him. Rambler didn't seem bothered by it.

"I told you, Eddie's fine," Rambler said.

"Eddie," Gregory agreed, casting around for some way to resolve the height disparity. He ended up seating himself on the bench, which at least put them closer, though it still felt odd. "What are you doing out at this hour?" he continued.

"Oh!" Eddie said excitedly. "Fishing! The lake fish come up to feed at dusk."

Gregory cocked his head at him. "You were bowfishing?"

"I've been learning." Eddie jostled the bow slung over one shoulder. "Found out that the National Conservation guys, your park rangers? They teach classes in it at the lake east of the palace."

"We're very proud of our heritage," Gregory managed.

"You should be. I haven't had this much fun in years. You get your bow and you stand in a little boat like a stand-up paddleboard, and you push out onto the lake – and when the fish come up to feed, whap!" Eddie smacked the window ledge for emphasis.

"Yes, I…grew up here, we went bowfishing when I was a boy," Gregory said.

"I'll be honest, I didn't think it'd work," Eddie said. "But check it out!"

He flicked the bag off his shoulder and lifted it up. It turned out to be a wicker basket, containing several fish. They were average size, plump from the bounty of springtime in the lake. They looked healthy, which pleased Gregory as a monarch, and there were a respectable number of them with only small wounds, which impressed him as a sportsman.

"That'll show me to be skeptical," Eddie said, shouldering the basket again. "Anyhow, I'm gonna clean these while they're fresh and pack them in ice for Simon. Maybe do a late-night fish fry. Hey, have you eaten?" he asked, brow furrowing. "Getting late, Your Highness."

"A few hours ago," Gregory said. "I was just – "

"Great!" Eddie interrupted, and started *climbing through the window*.

It was just far enough off the ground to be difficult, but even as Gregory went to help him through, he hauled himself up and swung his entire body over the ledge, in a move more reminiscent of a parkour video than a cooking demonstration. Gregory blinked at him as he slid lightly over the sill and into the office.

"Hope security doesn't come after me for that," Eddie said, dusting himself down.

"We don't have guards on the windows," Gregory replied.

"Probably to your credit, means nobody wants to kill you that badly," Eddie said, heading for the door that led out into the hallway. "Come have some fish with me."

"I…if you insist," Gregory managed, following as Eddie made a beeline for the kitchen.

Once there, Gregory made his way to a stool at the prep table as Eddie settled his fishing bow in the corner and bustled around, digging out knives and bowls. He put a pot on the stove and poured oil into it, heating the oil while he gutted the fish deftly.

"You look like you've done this a lot," Gregory observed after a while, for lack of anything else to say.

"Oh, yeah," Eddie said, sleeves rolled up, muscles in his forearms flexing as he worked. "I used to sling fish at a fry shack. I could probably do this in my sleep."

"Sounds like a difficult job."

Eddie gave him a curious look as he laid the fish out in a neat row on a prep tray and began filleting two of the biggest. "Not usually what people say when I tell them that. Fry cooks don't get the kind of respect TV stars do."

"Well, there's hot oil involved, which as a royal I'm very familiar with," Gregory said, and Eddie's jaw dropped.

"Was that a joke about boiling oil?" he asked, delighted. "Where'd you pull that out of?"

"When you're attending boarding school and they know your father's a king, you get all kinds of good material," Gregory told him. "My friends used to call coming over to my room for evening study *storming the castle*."

"Wild. Did you get Vlad the Impaler jokes?"

"Mm, no, I think we're too Mediterranean for that," Gregory said. "One of my teachers called me Prince Charming for a year, though."

"That's equally wild but way less cool," Eddie said.

"How so?" Gregory asked.

"Not cool for teachers to do it, that's punching down. Kids don't need that kinda stress."

"It wasn't terrible. It was good-natured, and if I couldn't hold up to that, I'd never hold up under all this," Gregory said thoughtfully. He'd never thought much of the ribbing he'd gotten over being a prince; it was just people who didn't fully understand the situation and were probably trying to process the strangeness of his existence. But it was a little nice to see someone having sympathy for the mortified fourteen-year-old Prince Charming.

"Uneasy lies the head, eh?" Eddie asked kindly, whisking something in one of the bowls. Gregory looked at him in surprise, startled as much by the literary reference as by a sudden return to reality from his thoughts.

"It kinda spoils my schtick, but I *can* read," Eddie added, grinning over his shoulder. "And Shakespeare was low entertainment for rude mechanicals, so I guess it's on brand."

"It's from one of the histories, though, isn't it?" Gregory asked, hoping it wasn't from *Macbeth*.

"*Henry the Fourth, Part Two: The Empire Strikes Back*," Eddie agreed.

"No, part two would be *Attack of the Clones*," Gregory said thoughtfully.

Eddie let out a startled laugh, almost dropping the fish he'd been about to put in the batter. He set the fillets down and turned to Gregory.

"That is the nerdiest thing I've ever heard royalty say," he declared, pointing at Gregory. "You just had that right there at the front of your brain."

"In my defense, Alanna really loves the prequels," Gregory said, which set Eddie off again. He laughed his way through battering the fillets and laying them carefully into the oil, then set the old wind-up timer Simon kept by the stove.

"Do you like Shakespeare?" Gregory asked, curious now.

"Usually I joke that I've just spent a lot of time in parks," Eddie said. Gregory frowned. "Because Shakespeare's always happening in a park somewhere?"

"It takes an unusual level of dedication to see *Henry IV part 2*," Gregory said. "It's not really park fare."

"Man, this is *really* going to spoil my schtick," Eddie said, washing his hands and gathering up a mesh straining spoon, big enough to scoop out the fish with. "There's a reason I went into TV, my friend. I majored in theatre." He put a dramatic flair on the last word, bowing regally. "Of the thirty-nine-ish plays of Shakespeare, I've seen thirty-six."

"Which ones are you missing?"

"Well, I've never seen *The Winter's Tale*, that's just bad timing on my part. I've never been sober for all of *Titus Andronicus*, so I don't know if that counts. And I've never seen *Twelfth Night*."

"*Twelfth Night*? Really? Isn't that one *required* to happen in parks?" Gregory asked. He could recall seeing at least three versions of it. Even his cousin Jerry liked *Twelfth Night*. He called it a banger.

"I've been saving it for a special occasion," Eddie said. "I mean, I've read it, I know what it's about. But like, I saw *Hamlet* three times in two years for school, more if you count all the movie versions I had to watch. Do you know how boring *Hamlet* gets?"

"Some would say it begins boring," Gregory said.

"Well, I didn't want to ever be the kind of douchebag who thinks, *Man, Twelfth Night again?* I want it to have the preciousness of rarity," Eddie finished, flipping the fish deftly in the oil. "I'm going to wait until I hear about a really great production of it and also it's my birthday or something, and then I'll just go all out with it."

"That's an oddly charming idea," Gregory said.

"Thanks, I'm full of 'em," Eddie replied with a grin. "Does Askazer-Shivadlakia have a state theatre or anything like that?"

"That was good, you didn't even have to look at your hand that time," Gregory pointed out, amusement in his tone taking the sting out of the words.

"Thanks, I've been practicing," Eddie replied.

"We have a small national theatre, but it's mainly for cultural preservation. Most of the arts in the country are independent. We subsidize a lot through grants, but there are constraints on how far the government can dictate how the money is used."

"Guess I asked the right guy," Eddie said. "Well, I can't advise you to fund any of the histories and most of the tragedies end badly for the kings, but the comedies have some decent princes."

"I'll bear that in mind."

"I suppose it's a lot, running a country," Eddie mused, poking the frying fish. "I mean, you must know that kind of information for everything that happens around here."

"Some of it I outsource," Gregory said, as Eddie scooped the fish onto a sheet of brown paper he'd found. "And if I didn't want the job I wouldn't have taken it."

"Aren't you kind of obliged, though?" Eddie asked, salting the fillets and tearing the paper into pieces to wrap them in. "Malt vinegar?"

"Probably, somewhere," Gregory replied, gesturing at the pantry.

"Helpful." Eddie rummaged in a rack of bottles nearby. "Aha!"

"Askazer-Shivadlakia is a democratic monarchy," Gregory continued. "Power doesn't automatically pass within families. The king has to be confirmed by a popular vote. The kind of personality who wants to be king tends to run in families, so it's convenient that I'm the king's child and wanted the job, but if I hadn't we'd just have held a general election."

"Wait, so you're *elected*?" Eddie asked, disbelieving. "That's *beyond* wild."

"It's not really different from electing a president, although the scale is smaller, of course," Gregory said. He'd developed a little patter for this explanation years ago, around the time he had seriously started considering election to kingship when his father retired. Eddie gathered up the fish in bundles and brought the bundles over to him as he explained. "We had a traditional monarchy, but one of our recent kings – Gregory II, actually, I'm named for him – saw what was happening in Russia just before the Revolution. He decided some pre-emptive democracy might be in order. A small country like ours needs stability and wants one person in office long-term, so generally rule is a life term once elected. But if the people don't like the king, it's possible to call a vote of no-confidence and a new election." He accepted the brown-paper bundle of fried fish Eddie offered, pulling a piece off to taste it. "That's very good. You can tell how fresh the fish was."

"Thanks. Hey, hang on," Eddie said, pulling out his phone. "Say cheese."

Gregory huddled behind his fish a little, trying to show it off as the real star.

"Can't hurt that you're photogenic," Eddie said, setting the phone aside and biting into his own fish dinner. "Has a king ever actually been voted out?"

"Gregory II's son was voted out," Gregory said. "He lost to my grandfather."

"He lost to…so you're named for a guy you're not related to?" Eddie asked.

Gregory swallowed a mouthful of the succulent, crisp-crusted fish before replying. "Our sense of tradition is strong. He's a spiritual ancestor, anyway. Reminder to be a good king."

"Tell us, Crown Prince Gregory, what makes a good king?" Eddie asked, holding out his fish like a microphone. Gregory smiled.

"A strong head for detail," he said. "Empathy, diplomacy, statesmanship. And since I'm elected I do have to be at least a little popular. Have to mind my manners. No boiling oil. Except for fish."

"No boiling oil is a pretty low bar to clear," Eddie replied.

"It does take more effort than that," Gregory admitted, as Eddie set the rest of his fish aside and picked up his phone again. "I'm not…really a natural at the likability part."

Eddie frowned down at his phone. "Well, they voted for you, so you can't be too bad at it."

"Hadn't thought of it that way," Gregory said, pondering this. He'd thought of it more like…a force of nature. He was of age and wanted the job, and he was the king's son, so it was easier for the voters to simply let it happen. The idea of people voting for him because he was well-liked, rather than convenient, was a novel thought.

"Is it okay if I upload this?" Eddie asked, flashing the phone at him to show the photo he'd taken. It wasn't half-bad, even if less of it was of the fish and more was of him than he'd hoped. His hair looked fine, and he was giving what Alanna called the Smolder with his eyes. "Comms said I could upload any photos taken personally, as long as everyone gave verbal consent. The fish think I should," Eddie added, pointing to the now nearly-empty cone of paper with a smile.

"I suppose," Gregory said. "You'd know better than I would, it's your Photogram."

"Prince Gregory…strong…Photogram game," Eddie said aloud as he typed, then looked up. "Any opinion on the fish?"

"I should probably make some kind of comment about fried fish being a sometimes food," Gregory said thoughtfully.

"It's fish! It's good for you. Omega-3s and all that."

Gregory grinned at him. "Hashtag truly-tasty?"

"Ah, you've been reading my posts!" Eddie shook a finger. "A good catchphrase is worth its weight in gold, especially as a hashtag, but it's all just showmanship. I'm postin' this without any scolding about fried food."

"Fair enough," Gregory replied. "I really should get back to work."

"Well, I'm a fry cook who majored in theatre so I'm not qualified to manage affairs of state," Eddie said. "But I think you should know, fish fried by me is the highlight of any day. It can only go downhill from here. So if you want to get some sleep – and buddy you look good but you do look tired – I think you should throw in the towel."

"You'll be my excuse, eh?" Gregory asked.

"There's photographic evidence of it on the internet," Eddie said solemnly.

He was tired, and the food was warming; he felt like his shoulders had dropped a few inches just from the last half hour.

"All right," he agreed. "Next time, though, I won't be bribed by fish."

"I'm sure I can come up with something," Eddie said. "Sleep well, Your Highness!" he added, calling after Gregory as he left the kitchen.

He made it to his bedroom, left most of his clothes on the floor, and fell into bed, asleep almost as soon as his head hit the pillow.

SIX WEEKS UNTIL
THE CORONATION OF HIS MAJESTY
KING GREGORY III

"GOOD MORNING, READERS and friends and everyone who is keeping it new!" Eddie said into the phone camera. It was being carefully held by Simon, who had foolishly allowed himself to be roped into it.

Eddie felt good, and he knew he showed it. He'd been plotting this for days, but he'd been a little surprised when Alanna agreed to his plan. He suspected she'd said yes so readily in part because she could see the tired, drawn look on the prince's face as easily as he could.

"I'm blown away by the hospitality of Askazer-Shivadlakia – take that, haters, I finally learned to say it – and I'm going to showcase some of that for you today," he continued. "People love their food here and they love to show it off!"

He held up a slice of the fish salami, which was…well, it was certainly new, he told himself.

"But I've worked my way through all of the cured meats, so I think fans of the show know what that means…" he blew air through his lips in a staccato drumroll as he flung the salami aside. "It's time for cheese!"

Simon very patiently kept the phone still while Eddie waved his arms in the air, miming like he was at a football game, cheering wildly.

"But cheese is too good to eat alone," he continued. "I love to share a plate. And when you're planning a shindig like the coronation banquet, you have to know what the belle of the ball wants. So stay tuned to Photogram today! As soon as I'm done filming this, I'm going to go find Crown Prince Gregory and convince him to come with me!"

Simon, otherwise unflappable, looked up from the camera screen and said, "What?" in a voice full of shock, outrage, and delight.

Eddie, knowing it didn't get funnier than that, reached out and took the phone, ending the recording.

"Are you really going to interrupt the prince's day for cheese?" Simon demanded, as Eddie threw a million hashtags on the video and posted it immediately.

"Well, I'm gonna try," Eddie said, pocketing the phone. "Wanna come see me work?"

"I should have made popcorn," Simon replied, following him down the hallway. They could hear the prince's voice in his morning briefing; Alanna, standing just outside the doorway at the back of the crowd, gave a little wave when they approached.

"…discuss this again after the coronation," the prince was saying. "In the meantime, if my father tells you something different, it is still his kingdom. If you're concerned about conflicting orders, speak to Alanna, she'll make the final determination. Alanna?"

"Here, Your Highness," Alanna called.

"Keep me in the loop on any miscommunication."

"Never happier," she replied, to scattered laughter.

"All right, everyone's dismissed," Gregory said, and people began to file out, a few nodding at Eddie or Simon as they left. Alanna stepped into the office, and Eddie put his head in the doorway.

"Ah, Eddie! And Simon. Did you need something?" Gregory asked. "It's only that I have two minutes before a two hour meeting."

"I'm going to say something you're not going to like, and that is this: Ditch it," Eddie said.

Gregory laughed. "I wish, but it's vital. If you can't cover it before the meeting, maybe email me a summary? Or talk to Alanna, she's good at condensing."

"Nah," Eddie said.

"…nah?" Gregory asked, raising his eyebrows.

"Ditch the meeting, come to town with me. I need your opinion on cheese."

"It's a major export but a luxury brand, so we can't depend on it for revenue," Gregory said promptly. "If the economy tanks we all eat very nice cheese nobody else will buy, but the crown will need to subsidize the producers."

"You could be eating very nice cheese in ten minutes without an economic recession," Eddie said.

"Affairs of state – " Gregory began, but there was a soft beep from his phone. He looked down at it, frowning, then up at Alanna.

"Did you just cancel my meeting with the Agricultural Cabinet?" he asked Alanna.

"I had one of those in college," Eddie said to Simon, who nodded sagely. "Great for growing tomatoes."

"No, the meeting's still happening, I just removed you from it," Alanna said. There were two more beeps. "And the follow-up briefing, and the accounting re-evaluation meeting after that."

"I created that meeting," Gregory said.

"No, you requested it, I created it, which means I can kick you out whenever I want."

Gregory rubbed his eyes. "Al, I can't get off on the wrong foot with my entire Agricultural Cabinet."

"I know," she said. "I'm bringing in the duke. He's not doing anything, and they all like him."

"Jerry's never doing anything, and he exists to be liked," Gregory said. "He's not going to understand one word in three they say to him."

"But I will, and I can condense it for you," Alanna said. "Greg. This is your last few weeks before you're king. Go have some fun." He opened his mouth, but she barreled onward. "All the crops and their statistics will still be here after the coronation, and so will all the meetings. You need a day."

He looked back and forth from Alanna to Eddie, and Eddie could tell when he realized this had been planned.

"All right," he said, standing and spreading his hands in defeat. "Let's go. Show me this amazing cheese."

"Triumph!" Eddie crowed. Gregory followed him out of the office, Alanna locking up behind them. Simon headed for the kitchen, and Eddie held the door to one of the side entrances of the palace, which would set them on a footpath down to the main street of town.

Once they were out of sight of the palace, Eddie dug in his bag and pulled out a hat, passing it over. It was bright blue and said TRULY TASTY in tie-dye patterned embroidery on the front. The prince accepted it, perplexed, and once his hands were full Eddie placed a pair of blue cat's-eye sunglasses on his face.

"What is this?" Gregory asked, pulling the glasses off to inspect them.

"I got you a disguise," Eddie said. "Glad I didn't have to talk you out of wearing the uniform with all the braid and stuff, actually. Can't have you mobbed while we're in town."

"Eddie, I'm the prince of a country with a smaller population than Manhattan," Gregory answered, but he did put the hat on. "People are going to know it's me." His phone beeped again and he frowned at it. "Did you post about this on Photogram?"

"Well, a lesson I happen to have learned in Manhattan is that if you look like you don't want to be recognized, most people will mind their own damn business," Eddie answered. "Of course people are going to know it's you, you're highly recognizable and built like a Greek god. This is a hint you want them to pretend they don't."

Gregory clearly didn't have a response for this, but he also clearly tried very hard. "Do you know, in theory the kings of Askazer-Shivadlakia are descended from Apollo?" he managed.

"Explains some things," Eddie said. "But you're not a hereditary king."

"Again, it's the spirit that counts," Gregory said, putting the sunglasses back on. Between the hat worn brim-forward like a nerd, the slightly askew glasses, and his upright royal posture, he gave the impression he was actively *trying* to seem awkward. "How do I look?"

"I haven't known you very long," Eddie answered, holding up his phone in selfie mode to show him his reflection, "but I feel confident in saying you've never looked less royal."

Gregory let out a startled bark of laughter at his own appearance. He reached out and tapped the photo button, preserving the image. "Do not post that to Photogram."

"No, that one's for the scrapbook," Eddie agreed, pocketing his phone again. "I'm not kidding about the cheese, though. Let me tell you my impressions so far and you can spout every fact you ever memorized about domestic cheese production."

The walk into town was educational. Eddie thought he'd learned a lot from talking to cheese mongers, but most of them were craftsmen who made small-batch cheese, or retailers who bought wholesale from the one large manufacturer, further inland, where most of the dairy farming was done. Neither group had the overhead view of things that the prince did, and they didn't want to. Eddie did; he liked to know how things worked, and he'd done very well for himself by making content that traced things back to their origins. He'd packaged it up in beach-bum slang and easily digestible sound bites, but it was all there.

Gregory knew the cost of everything his country produced, where it came from and where it went, but he also looked at all of it in terms of the passage of time. If the global economy suffered, what would happen to his people? If there was a sudden uncontrollable demand for some product his country produced, where could the supply chain be supported? Could local delicacies be made elsewhere and simply stamped with the royal seal? How long could that last before the assurance of quality that came with the king's seal was watered down?

"….which is why I think tax subsidy endowment accounts are so vital," Gregory said, as they arrived on the doorstep of the first cheese shop on Eddie's agenda. "It's a hard sell to people who don't understand endowment finance, though."

"I can imagine," Eddie replied. "And this was all super cool, but now I want you to try a thought experiment."

Gregory nodded, attention focusing.

"I want you to consciously attempt to forget that tax subsidy endowment accounts exist and think about how much you like good food," Eddie said. Gregory's brow knitted. "We're not here to judge the quality of king's-imprint domestic product. We're here to pick out some cheese you really like for a party you're super excited about."

"I think super excited would be an extremely generous term for my feelings on the coronation," Gregory replied.

"Thought experiment," Eddie reminded him. Gregory nodded and seemed to genuinely be making the attempt. Eddie pushed the cheese monger's door open. "All right. Come with me."

Alanna reflected, an hour into the Agricultural Cabinet meeting, that the downside of being the right hand of the prince, soon to be king, was that you had many of the same boring experiences he did without any of the luxury.

Not that Gregory lived extravagantly; King Michaelis and his son both had relatively simple tastes and preferred sport and statecraft to partying or lavish spending. The Queen had been more fond of the finer things in life, but even she hadn't been particularly fancy by royal standards. And Alanna had a title, or would when her grandmother passed, and she didn't even want that one.

But the point was that Alanna was in this meeting so Gregory wouldn't have to be, and nobody was calling *her* Your Highness.

On the other hand, she'd volunteered for this when Eddie suggested his plan to her, thinking Gregory could use both the time away from his desk and a little PR boost with the populace. Eddie Rambler had a golden touch; where he went, people followed, emotionally if not literally. He'd raised the profile of Askazer-Shivadlakia significantly. Even among their own people, being seen out with him could only be good for Gregory.

Her phone vibrated silently every so often and she kept an eye on Photogram, but as promised Eddie was being restrained. The photos he was posting were good quality, he always named the shop in the photograph, and so far nobody locally following the Photogram seemed to have caught up with them.

Jerry – more properly Gerald, 12th Duke of Shivadlakia – fidgeted in the chair next to her and tapped her phone with the cap of his pen.

"How's it going?" he mouthed.

"Seems fine," she whispered back. Jerry nodded and ostensibly turned back to the meeting. He was asking, if not especially well-informed questions, then at least not the most obvious ones. Jerry's family were old landed nobility from before Askaz and Shivadlakia had combined into a single country, and they had apparently bred for charisma. They had been kings, on occasion, but more often regents, and sometimes what Jerry referred to as evil advisors. Not that Alanna didn't have a few of those in her own history, she supposed.

Gregory's family on his father's side were relative newcomers, immigrants from only a handful of generations back, which was perhaps why they treated rule like a civic duty, while Jerry treated it like a quaint chore. Jerry could have stood for king if he'd wanted, but he preferred to make himself amiable and be otherwise useless. In that sense he was a good tool to have around the place. He could be deployed effectively against annoying bureaucrats, overly friendly grifters, squabbling government ministers, and once, memorably, a handsy ambassador bothering palace staff.

A shift in the air pressure of the room told her she'd missed something; people were stretching, speaking to one another, or rising to leave the room.

"Five minute break," Jerry said to her, cracking his neck. "Want me to see if I can stretch it to fifteen? You look like you could use a nap."

"No, my mind just wandered," she replied. "Did I miss anything vital?"

"I'll tell you later. It's all locked away up here," he added, tapping his temple.

"I'm sure there's empty space enough."

"You're a monster, Al," he informed her.

"Pain builds character," she replied ruthlessly. "Anyway, it's for Greg."

"Sure, you say that. I think you just want the chef to give you your own cooking show," Jerry said with a grin. "I know it's not just getting Gregory out of his office for a couple of hours. What's going on?"

Alanna shrugged. "I felt like he needed a reality check."

"Why?"

She sat back, staring up at the ceiling, relaxing while she could. "He wants me to find him a husband."

"Oh saints," Jerry cackled. "He has met you, right?"

"It's not that! I'd be extremely good at finding someone a husband. I have great taste in men and I'm highly efficient," she protested.

"Physician heal thyself, then."

"I don't want a husband, Jerry, I don't have time for one. The point is, the king's on him to get married for the good of the country, he's feeling a little raw about it, and he's busy. So he made me set up this husband-hunt meeting for after the coronation."

"Huh." Jerry slouched down next to her, contemplating this. "That's kind of sad."

"It's extremely sad and it's very out of touch in that dumb way he gets," Alanna sighed.

"He can be deeply stupid about other humans," Jerry agreed.

"So I thought if he got out and talked to someone who didn't work in politics for a few hours he'd maybe relax a little," Alanna said. She held up her phone, which was flipped to Eddie's latest post. It was, for the most part, just an anonymous pair of hands holding a large flat wheel of cheese. If she didn't know what Gregory had been wearing that morning or if she didn't recognize the insignia of the royal family of Askazer-Shivadlakia on his ring, she wouldn't know it was his hands holding the wheel. "He seems to be having fun."

"Well, then our suffering is not in vain," Jerry said. "Look out, better sit up straight, someone's coming to talk to us about figs."

It was afternoon by the time Eddie and Gregory said goodbye to the last of the cheese mongers and turned back towards the palace. Neither of them had bothered with lunch, but Gregory felt warm and expansive, pleased with what he'd seen and full of good food he'd sampled all morning. Eddie, who was carrying a messenger bag that was significantly heavier than it had been when they set out, whistled as they walked.

"You know, I think that was potentially more educational than the Agricultural Cabinet briefing would have been," Gregory said, enjoying the breeze off the beach below Fons-Askaz as they climbed the gentle incline back to the palace.

"See, I knew you'd have fun," Eddie replied.

"It's important. I want to be able to confidently speak about every aspect of our farm-to-table pipelines, and that naturally includes cheese," Gregory said, already organizing a campaign in his head – something to do with a line of exports, perhaps.

"And also you had fun," Eddie said. Gregory shot him a tolerant look.

"Yes, I also had fun," he agreed, removing the hat but keeping the sunglasses on.

"And we found some great food. Not sure what I'm doing with some of it yet, but nothing goes to waste in Simon's kitchen," Eddie said cheerfully.

"If nothing else, fondue's very popular here," Gregory said. "Might have a family dinner, invite in some of the cousins."

"That reminds me, I was curious," Eddie said. "Who's the duke that Alanna got to stand in for you today?"

"Ah, Jerry. His family's been in state politics forever. He and Alanna and I were thick as thieves as children. At school he was always a year ahead of me and making my teachers grateful I was so well-behaved. He gets into some small scrape about once a year to keep us humble, but he's very good at making other people feel important."

"He's not like...out for your job though, right?" Eddie asked. "I'm not in *Hamlet*, is what I'm asking."

"Well, we do live in a park. But no," Gregory assured him. "He's a good man on your side in a pinch. Sort of a big brother. Cousin on my father's side."

"It's good when family gets along," Eddie mused. "Especially when it's a family business, which I guess this government sort of is. My family does okay but I can't imagine the yelling we'd do if we had to rule a whole country."

"Are you all chefs?" Gregory asked, wondering what kind of family brought up a man like Eddie.

Eddie burst out laughing. "Oh, no. Most of my family work in Dad's auto shop. Those that work at all, anyway."

"Auto shop!" Gregory blinked at him.

"Sure. My dad specializes in trucks and does van art on the side. His sister works on beach buggies that my mom rents out from her surf shop."

"You have a pedigree I was wholly unaware of," Gregory observed, staggered by this information.

"Yeah, they put it in the puff pieces whenever someone needs a bio of me but it doesn't come up a lot," Eddie said. "They're all pretty free spirits. They don't like a lot of attention, so I try to keep them out of the spotlight."

"And you didn't care for that life?" Gregory asked.

"Well, I had a great childhood. All that stuff's awesome when you're ten and someone else is driving. I like surfing, and I'm okay with an engine. But I got older, wanted something different." Eddie shrugged. "I had bigger dreams than opening a taco stand next to the surf shop."

"I suppose we're opposites, in a way," Gregory said.

"How so?"

"I bought into the family tradition. You climbed out. Nothing wrong with that, just…different."

"I don't think it's opposite, exactly," Eddie replied, frowning – more like he was puzzling it out than like he disagreed. "You wanted to be king, didn't you? Nobody pressured you?"

"No," Gregory said. "Father has always said it's a job you have to choose, and my mother agreed. I could have gone into business or law, or – I suppose I could have opened a taco stand, though I don't think they'd have been delighted by that."

"So we both saw what we wanted, and we both looked at the consequences of reaching for it and accepted them," Eddie said. Gregory considered this as the palace came into view at the end of the road.

"That's…true," he allowed. "I have strong feelings about this place. I saw how hard my parents worked to protect it. It's a noble calling, at least I think so. And I like it, too."

"I gotta say I never thought of 'television chef' as a noble calling," Eddie said, as they drew closer to the palace. "But it's kinda how I treated it anyway. I knew kids who wanted to be famous but I didn't want fame, exactly. I just wanted to talk to a lot of people about something I really loved. Fame's mostly one of those consequences."

"Huh," Gregory said.

"What?"

"You're right, I don't think we are opposites." He took the sunglasses off, leaning against the lintel of the doorway into the palace. "And I had better go deal with the consequences of the Agricultural Cabinet."

"I'm glad you could come out today," Eddie said. Gregory held out the sunglasses and hat, but Eddie waved a hand.

"The merch is free. Hold onto it for the next time you need to ditch," he said.

Gregory felt unaccountably touched by this; not only the gesture of finding him a ridiculous, useless disguise, but offhandedly giving it as a gift, and implying there might be another need for it in the future.

"That's kind, thank you," he said.

"Pay you twenty bucks to wear the hat instead of the crown at coronation," Eddie added, and Gregory laughed.

"I'm afraid I can't oblige that one. I hear the host of this show is a real beach bum."

"Yeah, well, wish me luck, this beach bum has a bunch of menus to present to his uptight new boss on Monday," Eddie replied. Even the ribbing for being a little uptight felt kind, like he knew Gregory didn't get much friendly teasing anymore.

"I'm sure I'll have some commentary on your Photogram posts to review by then," Gregory said. With a wave he ducked inside, leaving Eddie enjoying the sun on the palace steps.

Thirty seconds later, as Gregory was entering his office, his phone beeped. Eddie was posting to his Photogram, a selfie in the garden. It was captioned "Can't believe I just forgot to get a selfie with Crown Prince Gregory in a *Truly Tasty* hat. Letting you down, guys, it won't happen again."

Gregory tapped the image to Like it, making little hearts dance around the text, and then headed to the conference room to find Alanna.

FIVE WEEKS UNTIL
THE CORONATION OF HIS MAJESTY
KING GREGORY III

EDDIE WAS REALLY getting to like the palace of Askazer-Shivadlakia. It wasn't just that he had a cool room with a great view of the grounds, or that it was full of art and interesting people. It was that it felt like a home in a way a lot of places didn't. He'd cooked for celebrities in their mansions, he'd cooked in museums and on sound stages and even in a couple of what, in America, passed for castles. But most big institutional buildings, even if he liked them, just felt a little soulless. They were event spaces, not homes.

The palace here was different – it was a working building, the decor incidental to the real business of governing. The kitchens were beautiful (Simon's doing, he felt sure) and the hallways were draped in tapestries and lined in slightly worn rugs that softened the feel of stone underneath. And all of that was for a purpose, not for show.

He'd spent most of the morning in the kitchen with Simon, putting the finishing touches on his lunch presentation to the prince, going over checklists and the printed menu copies to make sure nothing was missing. Now the cold food was packed in a cooler and the hot food in a basket lined with tea towels, and he hummed cheerfully to himself as he gathered them up, making his way towards the prince's office.

"Eddie!" a voice called, and he turned in time to see the prince himself emerging from a conference room.

"Your Highness," he called back, waiting for Gregory to catch up with him. He had a tablet under one arm and was dressed the least formally Eddie had ever seen him, in a t-shirt and worn dark trousers. "Casual Monday?"

"Wh – oh," the prince looked down at his clothes. "I was getting fitted for the formal robes this morning, and they're dusty – they warned me to wear old clothes." As if to demonstrate, he sneezed, and a light flurry of powder floated off him. Eddie, without thinking, shifted the basket to the same arm holding the cooler, and brushed Gregory's shoulders clear of the remainder. "Thank you," Gregory said, dusting the rest of himself down. Eddie patted him on the shoulder, enjoying the muscle underneath briefly, and then rebalanced himself, cooler in one hand, basket in the other.

"I hear there's a good drycleaner in town," Eddie said, as they turned to Gregory's office. "I don't know if they do royal robes."

"Apparently the dust is part of the tradition," Gregory replied. "Is that samples in your basket?" he asked hopefully. "I haven't had lunch yet."

"It is, and it's both still hot," Eddie held up the basket, "and still cold," he continued, holding up the cooler, "so we should hustle."

"I've had some thoughts about those cheeses," Gregory said, and Eddie cheered a little internally.

"Me too!" he said, as Gregory led the way into his office. "I'm looking forward to – "

Eddie broke off, because Gregory had stopped a few paces inside the door. There was a man sitting in one of the office's guest chairs, book in one hand; even if his face wasn't on half the currency in the country, Eddie would have noticed his resemblance to Gregory. This was Michaelis, the current king. He'd just gotten accustomed to thinking of the prince as Gregory, and the renewed awe for the grandeur of Askazer-Shivadlakia's royalty filled him.

"Father," Gregory said, sounding both surprised and annoyed.

"Good morning," King Michaelis said, putting away the book he'd been reading. "Mr. Rambler, I presume. Pleasure to meet you."

"Your Majesty," Eddie said, remembering his manners. "The pleasure's mine."

"What are you doing here?" Gregory asked.

"Well, I know Alanna marked me as optional on the meeting invite, but for all your jokes it's not like I actually have died," Michaelis said. "This is almost as much my party as it is yours, in a way, and your mother used to like having me do the gala catering sampling with her. I thought I'd offer my opinion."

"Sure you didn't just want more of those meatballs?" Gregory asked. Eddie chuckled, which drew both their attention, a fearsome thing in itself. "Eddie, are there enough samples?"

"Sure, the more the merrier," he said, sidling past Gregory to begin unpacking the food onto the desk. Gregory sat down in the other guest chair. Eddie decided to stand, just in case sitting in the presence of the king was a political thing.

"I heard about your trip into town for cheese-sampling," Michaelis continued, speaking to Gregory as Eddie unpacked. "I thought I'd see if it was productive." He turned to Eddie. "Obviously the reception is extremely important, but the palace trusts you to produce a good meal without too much guidance. I want to make sure Gregory's time isn't taken up with incidentals. It's easy to be distracted from affairs of state. Such as the Agricultural Cabinet," he drawled at his son.

"Great for growing tomatoes," Eddie tried again, but the joke still fell flat. He wondered if he could get away with making it a weed joke instead. Not in front of the king, that was for sure.

"It's fine, once or twice," Michaelis said. "Everyone thinks it was charming of you to go yourself, and Gerald handled the cabinet competently. I just want to make sure it was worth it."

"So, I have four menus," Eddie said, because there wasn't any great place for that conversation to go, and Gregory seemed tense. "We can mix and match the foods a little depending on what you like." He handed the four printed menus to the king, who set them on the desk to share with his son. "On one end of the scale we have my personal favorite, the hot sandwich bar with passed apps, which we've already discussed a little. On the other end is a multi-course royal meal *a la russe*, with personal service by the waitstaff. Let me introduce you to some herbed clay pot chicken on peasant bread rolls."

He'd crafted his menus with local food in mind, but Alanna had made him well aware that the prince also wanted modernity. He hadn't counted – and clearly neither had Gregory – on the king joining them, and Eddie had no idea what the man's tastes were, other than what he'd gleaned from Simon's standard dishes. But all the food was good, which went a long way towards satisfying even the most exacting of parents, and Eddie had thought to bring a bottle of wine from the country's highlands ("Well…highland, there's just the one mountain," the wine merchant had explained) which smoothed the way a little more.

Going through the menus and the various hot and cold dishes that accompanied them, Eddie decided the tension between father and son probably wasn't normal. He prided himself on being a pretty good judge of character, and Michaelis didn't seem like a bad dad, or Gregory a disappointment. This was something else, which meant that until it came to a head he, at least, could probably safely ignore it. Maybe they would do the same.

So he kept serving and talking, two things he was good at, and ignored the vague elephant in the room. Still, he breathed a little sigh of relief when they finally reached the end of the presentation.

"I think if nothing else we've established something pretty vital," Gregory said, having finished off the last of the dessert nibbles.

"What's that?" his father asked, waving away Eddie's offer of a top-off on his wine.

"It's going to be great food regardless," Gregory said. "This was delicious, Eddie, thank you."

"It was good," Michaelis agreed. Both he and Gregory saw the 'but' coming, Eddie thought. "But the quality of the food is expected. It's only one aspect."

Gregory looked annoyed, but Eddie cut off a potential fight. "I'd love to hear your thoughts on that," he said sincerely, not moving to tidy away the plates or containers of food.

"The coronation is a ritual as much as an event. Everything about it should be a unified whole – dare I say a *magical* event, without getting too flowery about it," Michaelis said. "We call ourselves kings at this point, at least in part, because we have a cultural love of pageantry. We want things to look their best and impress those around us."

"I want that as well," Eddie replied. "Do you see anything in what I've shown you here that you think fits in best?"

"Well, I can't say I'm thrilled with the idea of a hot sandwich bar," Michaelis said.

"Yeah, the prince wasn't either," Eddie agreed. He shot Gregory a grin, a hint to stay calm, because he was looking more annoyed by the second.

"Smacks of a Las Vegas buffet," Michaelis continued.

"There's a time and a place for that style of service," Eddie replied. "Maybe this isn't it."

"I like it," Gregory said, a little sharpness creeping into his voice. "The family feeling of it. Maybe not the format, but..."

"This is an affair of state," Michaelis said.

"Yeah, but Dad, I can't stand the formal dinner thing. *You* don't even like it."

"No, but I had to learn to live with it to keep others happy. You might too. Not to say it has to happen at your coronation," Michaelis said, making a calming gesture with one hand. "But the coronation will set a tone."

"Exactly! I want us to seem approachable as well as impressive. A six-course meal is nobody's idea of a good time even with food this good. Too much sitting down."

Michaelis, to his credit, seemed to consider this. "And nobody likes a compromise."

"No," Gregory agreed. Both men looked at Eddie, who nodded as if he was considering this deeply. A good eighty percent of being a television host was looking like you were actively listening.

"I'm not out of ideas yet," he said, although he *absolutely was*. To cover, he started cleaning up the desk.

"These recipes – the flavors are great," Gregory said. "Don't throw the food out just because the look isn't right yet."

"But I do urge you to find a balance between informality and elegance," Michaelis said. His phone beeped. "And I'm afraid that's my afternoon appointment with the royal librarian."

"Need a book recommendation?" Eddie joked.

"Apparently I'm expected to dictate my memoirs," Michaelis said sourly. "Gregory, I'll see you at breakfast tomorrow."

He leaned over and kissed his son on the forehead, a seeming conciliatory gesture, and left. Eddie slowed his cleaning, waiting for Gregory to speak first.

"I am so, so sorry my father ambushed you," Gregory said finally.

"Sounds like he ambushed both of us, but it comes with the job," Eddie replied.

"Oh, for me too, I guess."

"Are you okay?" Eddie asked carefully.

"What?" Gregory replied.

"Well, obviously it's tough. He looks like he's feeling iffy about you playing hooky with me for cheese."

"He'll be fine. He's just worried about the coronation, like me. It's coming out in weird ways. You're not seeing him at his best."

"I'm not sure I made a great first impression," Eddie said.

"I'm guessing you have a lot of experience defying first impressions," Gregory replied, and Eddie laughed.

"Sure, that's true, I'm really more of a second-look kind of guy."

"Anyway, it's not his decision. Ultimately, it's mine, and whether or not he likes you, I do. So he'll have to put up with it."

Eddie smiled, genuinely touched. In show business it was rare for someone to stand so firmly behind anyone else. "Thanks. That means a lot – "

He had closed the basket on the pile of dishes, and was just picking up the cooler when Gregory held up a hand.

"By the time we get to the reception, I'll be king," Gregory said.

"Yeah?" Eddie replied, confused.

"It hits you in waves," he said. He let his hand drop to rest on Eddie's arm. "You realize what'll be different, and…that morning I'll be crown prince, and that evening I'll be king. The mistakes will be mine to make, so I guess…don't worry about my father. I'm on your side."

"I think I'm supposed to be on your side," Eddie reminded him. Gregory looked down at his hand and pulled it back slowly.

"Well, that's probably a question for the philosophers," he said. "Anyway. Just do some thinking, maybe build another few menus – will you have time?"

"All I got is time, baby," Eddie grinned. "Sure. I'll knock his socks off next time."

"And if my dad doesn't like my coronation banquet, the world won't end."

"Yeah, but it'll be uncool, and I'm here to prevent that."

"I'm reliably told I'm uncool anyway," Gregory said. "Do you need help getting that back to the kitchen?"

"Nope, it's fine." Eddie gave him the peace sign as he left. "I'll keep it new for you, boss!"

"That's Prince Boss to you!" Gregory called. Eddie chuckled, but by the time he made his way back to the kitchen he was more thoughtful.

Whatever Gregory said, this was clearly both a big deal and a significant problem. At this point more than Eddie's professional pride was on the line; besides, he'd given up on professional pride when he did that special where he had to do a kick line with a bunch of sports mascots. He wanted Gregory to enjoy his coronation, and impress his guests and his dad.

"How was it?" Simon asked, looking up from his dinner preparations when Eddie walked in.

"So-so," Eddie said thoughtfully. "Little soon to tell."

"What went wrong?" Simon inquired.

"Nothing wrong, exactly. King came to the tasting," Eddie said, unpacking the cooler and shoving leftovers into the big fridge. "He wasn't big on what I had to show."

"Not the food, surely. He knows good food, and yours is good," Simon replied.

"Thanks – no, the sandwich bar idea. He said it smacked of a Vegas buffet."

"I've had very good meals at buffets in Las Vegas," Simon replied.

"When the hell were you in Las Vegas, Chef?"

"I wasn't sprouted in Askazer-Shivadlakia, you know. If you want to learn about gourmet food, there are many places to study. When I was young I was offered Las Vegas or Paris, and I don't like Paris," Simon told him.

Eddie turned to stare at him. "You're French," he said.

"What has that to do with anything? You come from California, do you love Los Angeles?"

He had a point, and Eddie made a face to acknowledge it. Simon smiled.

"You had three other menus," Simon continued. "None of them appealed?"

"Well, the prince doesn't want a formal meal. They've got real conflicting opinions on what they do want. I'm supposed to come up with something that's modern, traditional, innovative, and on-brand, all at once."

"This is a terrible burden for a man who earns his living on the internet," Simon said, mock-solemn.

"You make fun, but this is serious! I want to make a good impression." Eddie looked around. "You got any dishes I could wash?"

"Sink is full, if you want to, but the staff will do it later," Simon told him.

"I'll do it. Good for thinking, dishwashing."

"If you say so. I don't like dish soap, either," Simon said, turning back to the prep table. "I leave you to your thoughts."

Gregory didn't always eat dinner in the family dining room, and lately he hadn't been there much, preferring to take a plate up to his room or eat in his office. For dinner, Alanna had brought him a plate as a check-in, and he thought Simon had probably heard about the tasting to judge from the composition of the plate.

Simon had been their chef since he was a child and knew all his favorite comfort foods: Askazer twist-bread, roasted vegetables with fresh herbs from the kitchen garden, and a slice of spiced meat pie. Not too much of any one food, but altogether it had been very satisfying.

He decided it would be a nice break to stretch his legs and bring the plate back himself; gathering up the remains of the meal, he locked his computer and stepped out into the hallway. Previous kings looked down on him from paintings as he passed, but they were old friends, and anyway he knew most of their scandals and secrets. A perk of being raised a prince was a healthy disrespect for royalty, he supposed.

It was amazing how productive work and a good meal had raised his spirits. Everything seemed a little brighter this evening, and perhaps he didn't even need to put in a few more hours tonight. Nobody would die if he waited until tomorrow to complete his current work, and the idea of a good book before bed felt indulgent, inviting. Even the kitchen looked friendly, with a warm wash of yellow light spilling out into the hallway and the sound of voices inside.

He stopped to listen, wondering what they were talking about. It was like lying in the dark listening to your parents talk in the other room, as he'd often done at their fishing lodge when he was a child.

" – His Majesty is retiring for a reason," Simon was saying, his voice drifting out over the sound of spoons against pans. Gregory wondered what they were cooking – dinner had already been served, but he knew Simon preferred to eat later, after the family meal was served.

"He knows it's time for someone younger to take the reins, someone with more modern ideas, and Prince Gregory is ready."

"At least it seems like he's happy it's his son," Eddie answered. There was a soft noise, a sort of *fwoom*, and the brief smell of alcohol burning. "Nicely done."

"Thank you. My point is, perhaps the king doesn't handle this so well."

"That's what the prince said, yeah."

"So he takes it out on the food, maybe. Your food, I mean."

"Well, the food never did anything," Eddie replied. Gregory leaned against the wall, just outside the doorway. From here he could see Simon at the stove, tossing vegetables in a stir-fry. "Food's just there to be delicious," Eddie continued. "Kinda like me. Hey! I'm gonna put that on a t-shirt. *Food is here to be delicious, just like me.*"

"That's very funny," Simon intoned. "All this is temporary, anyway. It will all settle down. These things feel more important in the moment than they truly are."

"Yeah, probably."

"And Prince Gregory will be a fine king. Very popular already," Simon said. Gregory smiled to himself, pleased at the praise.

"I don't know anything about kinging, so I can't speak to that," Eddie said. "But he's a nice guy. Funny, when he forgets to be a prince. If he weren't a prince…"

"He'd likely still be in politics," Simon said.

"Well, maybe, but I meant, if he weren't a prince, about to be a king, I'd definitely consider asking him out."

Gregory blinked, shocked.

"Would you now," Simon asked, sounding amused.

"Sure, why not? Good looking man, pretty personable. If I met him in a bar I'd like him. He's probably got some princess from another kingdom lined up, though. Or maybe a Hollywood movie starlet," Eddie said. "Looks like that and royalty too? The ladies must be three-deep."

"One would think," Simon said drily.

"Anyway, I need to do some thinking," Eddie continued, leaving Gregory back in the earlier conversation, still in shock. "Maybe do some research. Like, royal traditions. We could base the meal in that."

"It would be interesting. I can tell you where to look."

"That'd be great," Eddie said.

"The palace library has several books of past chefs' recipes, there may be something in there on special events as well – "

Gregory, realizing he probably shouldn't get caught lurking in the doorway, turned to retreat; the movement shifted the plate in his fingers, and before he could recover he'd fumbled it right in the doorway, sending it crashing to the ground.

He startled as badly as both Simon and Eddie did; they looked over, immediately concerned, and Gregory gaped at them for a second, wordless.

"Prince Gregory!" Simon announced, at the same time Eddie said, "Oh, snap!"

"I…the plate," Gregory managed. "I was just bringing it back, it slipped – "

"Are you okay?" Eddie asked, as Simon pivoted smartly towards the little closet where the mop and broom were kept.

"Yes, I'm fine…" Gregory looked down at the fragments of china. "But the plate. It slipped."

"The palace has no shortage of plates, Your Highness," Simon declared, returning with the broom, gently nudging him with the handle to back up so Simon could sweep up the fragments.

"Come on in, take a load off. Have a snack," Eddie offered, taking his elbow to guide him into the kitchen.

"Oh, no, I should go," Gregory said distractedly. Eddie let go of his elbow, but his hand hovered nearby. "Simon, I'm so sorry – "

"No matter," Simon said easily.

"Thank you for sweeping it up," Gregory told him earnestly. Simon nodded, clearly bewildered by his behavior. "I'll get out of your way."

"That's not necessary – " Eddie began, but he was already out the door. He faintly heard Simon call, "Sleep well!" before he took the stairs up to his apartments two at a time.

When the prince was gone, Eddie took the dustpan from Simon and crouched, holding it while Simon swept the broken plate into it.

"What was that all about?" he asked, picking the silverware out of the debris.

"I've no idea. I suppose dropping the plate startled him," Simon replied.

"He doesn't seem the kind to get jumpy over a little broken crockery."

"No, he never has been," Simon agreed. "He well knows we have plenty of plates. It's not even the good china," he added with a sniff.

"Maybe the king isn't the only one who isn't handling the coronation well," Eddie mused. He lifted the dustpan and carried it to the big garbage bin in the corner.

"Mm, perhaps. Alanna mentioned he's been moody," Simon remarked. "I will have to take matters into my own hands."

"Lord, what does that even mean?" Eddie asked, fascinated.

"More regular meals and higher protein," Simon decided. "Also more oil and butter. I will make a cake. Sugar, good for energy. Good pastries, lots of chicken and beef, and desserts." Simon rubbed his hands together, pleased.

Eddie put the dustpan away and came to rest both hands on Simon's shoulders. "You are a chef after my own heart, LeFevre."

"Hey, all you friends and fans out there!"

Eddie's voice was a little tinny through the phone speakers. His usual bright, cheerful tone was tempered, but Gregory wasn't paying a lot of attention to that; he was mostly absorbed in his own thoughts. It was early, and he was still in bed, but his phone had told him Eddie posted a new video that morning, so he'd rolled over and opened it, curious.

"I hope everyone's still keeping it new," Eddie continued in the video. He did a full rotation with the phone, catching the sunlight on the front facade of the palace as well as the mist rising over the gardens. "Isn't it beautiful country? Reminds me of the California foothills. Whenever I feel like I'm in need of inspiration these days, I come out here and look around. Get it? Look around," he said, and spun the opposite direction to give another 360-degree view. It was endearingly ridiculous, which Gregory was beginning to suspect was Eddie's whole point. He was ridiculous, but it was an earnest ridiculous, and there wasn't a hint of self-deprecation in it. That was just how Eddie Rambler was and he didn't care who knew it or disliked it.

It served him right for listening at doorways, Gregory thought, not for the first time since he'd dropped the plate the night before. He'd fled to his rooms after the kitchen incident, and hadn't slept especially well, mortified at his own behavior and confused by his reaction to Eddie's remarks. It wasn't like he'd never heard anyone say he was handsome, or even that he was nice. But it was more often tabloids or random strangers saying it, not people he knew.

Definitely not people in that inbetween state Eddie occupied, somewhere between stranger and friend. Eddie knew him just well enough to like him, which was very flattering, but he hadn't read Gregory's press (condescending when he was younger, sometimes brutal after he came out, but you couldn't let that affect you). Eddie didn't know him personally well enough to know he was gay.

It was nice to be liked for himself, though. Some men liked the dream of being with a prince more than they liked the idea of actually going on a date with him. And some liked the novelty of 'a prince' more than the reality of 'Gregory'.

He didn't think of himself as someone people were attracted to, he supposed. He wasn't inexperienced, but he knew himself to be a little shy in social situations where he didn't have the diplomatic script to fall back on. The idea of an attractive, successful, interesting person like Eddie, who clearly could have his pick of partners, suggesting a date with Gregory – essentially a quiet bureaucrat – was just…weird.

Nice, though, Gregory thought, as the video of Eddie rolled on.

"You can see one of the closest farms, just over there, and I'm told all the dairy grazing is up that way. These are the winter pastures, closer in to the sea, so the cows are all up in summer pasture right now while it's still warm. And down here," Eddie turned again, pointing to the coast. "You can see the fishing boats coming in, and the ice trucks bringing fresh meat in along the coast road. And that mountain! I'm told they joke they just have a single highland, but what a view!"

Eddie whistled low, pointing to the high mountain rising behind the palace. Gregory grinned. The only joke as tired as "we've just got the one highland" was "you're not a local until you make the One Highland joke". Eddie was doing what he did on all his TV shows – arrive somewhere, make himself at home, and show off the local culture. Nice to see his country getting the Eddie Rambler treatment.

Perhaps he should ask Simon to gently let Eddie in on his secret. Could be a fun time.

"Slight setbacks recently, but I'm not worried," Eddie said in the video. "I know you all can't wait to see the shindig I throw for the new king, and I promise to document every moment I can of it, but right now we're still in the planning stages. Anyone who tells you the life of a professional chef is all chocolate tastings and kitchen tours is selling you a line. Still, if you love what you do, the hell with everything else, right? I'll get through it."

He looked contemplatively up at the mountain.

Gregory, suddenly frustrated, closed the app and let the phone fall into the blankets. There wasn't the slightest point in considering a fling with Eddie, let alone actually allowing one. He was an employee, technically, and neither of them had the time for personal pursuits at the moment. Gregory himself was trying to convince Alanna that a political arranged marriage was a good idea. And Eddie was…well, Eddie. If he was out, Gregory didn't think it was very far, and Gregory'd had enough of closets.

Eddie was a goofball who made dumb jokes, and he certainly wasn't appropriate for a king consort, which was the whole point of dating anyone at this point. An American television chef wasn't going to leave it all behind to co-rule Askazer-Shivadlakia, even if he did like the food.

Pointless. Eddie was simply a kind man who was nice to look at, and an amiable employee who would be gone in less than two months. Best leave him to menu-making and get back to the business of ruling.

Three days later all of that went to hell.

He wasn't sleeping well, or rather, he wasn't sleeping often. When he did sleep it was deep and thorough, but he'd wake restless, or have too much nervous energy to manage more than a few hours. He had actually gotten out ahead of most of his work the previous day, however, so that morning instead of going early to the office he put on a pair of old running shoes, some jogging shorts, and a long-sleeved shirt, and went out to do a lap of the grounds.

There was a pretty good trail that circled most of the palace gardens, with scenic views and packed dirt, excellent for running. The whole loop was a decent level run, long enough to test his endurance, and nobody was likely to be around at five in the morning –

Except Eddie Rambler, who almost sent him sprawling.

Gregory was finally getting out of his own head, zoned out and enjoying the run, when there was a movement ahead on his left and someone called, "Prince Gregory!"

He startled, nearly tripped, and skidded off the path to a stop, wide-eyed. The shape moving ahead resolved itself into Eddie Rambler, a blond-tipped shadow next to one of the ornamental cherry-blossom trees.

"Eddie," Gregory panted, leaning over to rest his hands on his knees. "You startled me."

"Sorry! I thought you saw me," Eddie said, holding up his hands in a show of innocence. A canvas bag hung off one wrist. "Didn't mean to interrupt your workout."

"It's fine, I need to catch my breath anyway," Gregory said, straightening.

"Nice morning for a run."

"Yes, I thought so. Do you run?"

Eddie laughed. "Only from the cops. I just kind of assumed it was a nice day for it."

"Most runners don't really differentiate, to be honest," Gregory said. "If the world hasn't ended, it's a nice morning for a run. Walk you back to the palace?"

"Sure, I'd be happy for the company," Eddie agreed, falling into step with him.

"I always seem to catch you sneaking back with treasure," Gregory said. "What is it this time, spear-hunting boars?"

"No, I – wait, you have wild boar?" Eddie asked, distracted.

"Is that good or bad?" Gregory asked.

"Could I seriously go spear-hunt wild boar in a royal forest? I think if I do they legally have to write a folk song about me, right?"

"Oh, ah. Maybe. You could, is what I mean, but I don't recommend it," Gregory said. "They're large and very angry. But yes, in theory."

"Have you?"

"Hunted boar? No. I feel that we've fallen into some kind of rabbit hole," Gregory added, wiping his face with his shirt. He glanced at Eddie, who seemed flustered. "So you weren't out hunting."

"I was down at the harbor, looking over the catch. I thought about suggesting a clambake for the coronation, but boy did I get told."

"Ah, yes," Gregory agreed. "Shellfish at a party is bad luck. Old superstition. Something to do with drowning. Or more likely, one too many parties where they got bad oysters. Also, definitely not kosher."

"Shame. Anyway, I didn't want to come back empty-handed, so I stopped at the butcher and got chicken wings. I figured I'd make my infamous Trash Tower."

"Should I ask?" Gregory inquired.

"Play your cards right and you can have some," Eddie replied. "Come up to the kitchen, I'll show you how it's made."

"I really shouldn't," Gregory said. "I have to change, and I have a full day ahead – "

"Won't take long, wings cook fast."

"It's just…" Gregory trailed off, unable to come up with a good excuse. He didn't especially want to come up with an excuse, was the problem.

"Look, I know your dad probably thinks I shouldn't take up your time," Eddie began.

"It's not that – "

"It's okay, I get it," Eddie said, still sounding very reasonable about it. "Tell you what, I'll bring you a slice when it's done, instead. It's definitely not appropriate for your coronation but that's not really why I'm making it."

Gregory paused, considering this, realizing he was simply being a coward. He had the time, his father's feelings on the chef weren't really all that negative and certainly weren't going to impact his own feelings, and he liked Eddie's company.

"No, I have time for anything called the Trash Tower," he said.

Eddie looked surprised. "Will it horrify Simon?" he asked, starting to walk again.

"Oh, it horrifies everyone," Eddie assured him.

"What goes into it?"

"It's really something you witness more than a recipe you can explain," Eddie replied.

Simon was in the kitchen when they arrived, but he was doing something complicated with dough; he gave them a nod when Eddie greeted them and placed an apple in Gregory's hand as he passed, but otherwise ignored them. Gregory settled himself at one of the prep tables while Eddie set his cargo down.

"I invented it when I was about twenty," Eddie said, going to the fridge and taking out a bowl of mashed potatoes from some previous meal, as well as some cooked vegetables. "It's mostly about the presentation, but it's also about feeding a bunch of hungry college students with whatever they bring you to cook. It's flexible, but there's a sort of platonic ideal, and it has thankfully been many, many years since I didn't have enough money to buy exactly what food I wanted."

"This is a dish with a platonic ideal," Gregory repeated, skeptical.

"Most dishes have a platonic ideal, but only the Trash Tower is brave enough to admit it," Eddie said. "Want to help?"

"Dare I?"

"Grate cheese," Eddie told him sternly, placing a block of cheese from the fridge and a grater in front of him.

"All of it?"

"Most of it. I'll let you know when to stop." Eddie went back to the bag he'd brought in with him, unloading not just chicken wings but also turkey sausages and an enormous bag of potato chips.

"Didn't figure they kept these in the palace," Eddie said, when he saw Gregory looking at the bag. "Keep grating," he added, opening the bag to let the air out and promptly crumpling it up to crush the chips.

"Yes, Chef," Gregory replied. Simon laughed from his pastries as Eddie began laying out chicken wings on a roasting pan.

"Anyway, the basic premise of my relationship to cooking is that there is a simple, satisfying way to make almost any food," Eddie continued. "Simon, the oven?"

"Still hot from the pastries," Simon replied.

"Awesome." Eddie set the oven temperature a little higher and returned to the wings, sprinkling them with seasoning. "Every time I make a recipe, especially if I'm developing it for a cookbook or an episode, I ask myself which parts are necessary, which parts people might not know. And I try to do something fun with it, so that people who do cook for fun won't see just another recipe for, I don't know, pot roast or lasagna."

"Keeping it new," Gregory said.

"That's it exactly." Eddie put the chicken in the oven and set a frying pan on the stove, swirling oil into it.

"It's a very…youth-culture friendly slogan," Gregory said. "Good marketing, I guess."

"Turned out to be."

"Didn't you come up with it for the TV show?" Gregory asked, surprised.

"Ah! No, the show came later. I didn't come up with it, anyway."

"Who did?"

"Technically a Chinese emperor," Eddie said, like that was the most normal thing in the world. "Ch'eng T'ang, in the 18th century. But I sound like a real new-age asshole when I put it that way. I got it from Ezra Pound."

That clarified absolutely nothing and opened several fascinating new avenues into the inner workings of Eddie's mind, but Gregory honestly wasn't sure where to start.

He finally settled on asking, "Did *he* get it from the Chinese emperor?"

"Yeah, more or less. There's a story about Ch'eng T'ang having a bathtub with an inscription on it about how necessary it was to renew yourself daily. It's meant to be a lesson in good government," Eddie continued, digging in the pots and pans and coming up with a bundt mold. "Pound read about it in a book on Confucian moral philosophy."

"Where'd you come across it?"

"Modernist theatre. Modernism is all about renewal, and they all say Pound said it first, and as we've established, he got it from Ch'eng T'ang. Now, on the one hand, Modernism could be super playful, which is kind of where I plant my own flag. On the other hand, you start edging into Futurism, at which point renovation, making it new, gets a lot more about like…clearing away rubbish, erasing the past. It all goes very Mussolini after that. Not here for it."

"A good lesson to take away," Gregory agreed.

"I think so. Still, the philosophy is pretty sound. I took it as a sort of personal slogan. I really like the idea of always being in renewal. You keep what's already there, you just change it up a little. Always have a solid ideal to adapt from. Then you know where to fall back to, if you have to."

"A very Shivadh sentiment," Simon remarked. Eddie began stir-frying the vegetables, and for a while the crackle of oil and sizzle of some sauce he was concocting drowned him out.

Gregory, his duty done to the cheese, watched as Eddie began assembling…whatever it was. The chicken roasted while the vegetables fried, and then the frying pan was set aside while Eddie mixed more garlic into the potatoes. Then the still-hot chicken wings were pulled from the oven and stripped, Eddie making soft *hah* noises over his singed fingers the whole time, and the meat tossed with the vegetables.

It came together with remarkable speed after that. Eddie laid a few remaining whole wings in the bottom of the bundt pan, then stirred up the potatoes and pressed a layer on top of the chicken. He alternated layers of potato, vegetables with chicken, cheese, slices of sausage, and crushed potato chips, until the cake pan was full and all the other pots and pans were empty. Then he carefully covered the pan with a platter, flipped it, and tapped out a perfectly molded mountain of food, topped with golden wings, oozing with melting cheese.

"Behold, the Trash Tower," Eddie said. "Ready for the finishing touch?"

"I'm intrigued and aghast," Gregory told him. Eddie picked up a bottle of hot sauce and striped it sparingly in one direction, then patterned mayonnaise across it, sprinkling the last of the potato chips over all of it.

"Bravo, that looks terrible," Simon observed.

"Take my picture with it, every time I make this people lose their minds," Eddie ordered, handing Gregory his phone with the camera open. Gregory lined up the shot of Eddie holding the Trash Tower, snapped a few for good measure, and then passed it back as Eddie set the platter down.

"My kingdom has never witnessed anything like it," Gregory said.

"Few have. Well, made by me, anyway. I published the recipe a few years ago and it's pretty popular for tailgating, apparently."

"Do you excavate it from the top down, or from the outside inward?" Gregory asked.

"Slice it," Eddie replied. He took a knife from the rack and cut two slightly wobbly slices, tipping them out into bowls, topping each with one of the whole chicken wings. "Simon, you in?"

"No, I have eaten, and I need to take the pastries in to the breakfast room. Shall I tell your father you've eaten also?" Simon asked Gregory.

"Thanks," Gregory said with a nod. Eddie offered him a fork and he dug it into the food in the bowl, trying to get a little of everything in one bite, instinctively understanding that was the best way to attempt this. Eddie watched him sample it, awaiting a reaction.

"Well, that's different," Gregory said thoughtfully, still chewing. "I like the crunch from the chips."

"I do a vegetarian version with mushrooms, too, and there's one with rice," Eddie said, starting on his own. "Some of my better work," he pronounced, after couple of mouthfuls. He leaned against the prep table, next to Gregory, and took out his phone, opening the photo app to study the pictures of him that Gregory had taken. "Oh hey, that's good work," he said, even as he cropped and color-adjusted the image.

"Easy subject," Gregory replied, between bites. It somehow tasted better the more you ate.

"I do my best," Eddie answered, amused, dropping the image into a Photogram post. He set his bowl down to concentrate on typing out a caption. "Trash Tower by Eddie Rambler, photograph by Crown Prince Gregory," he said as he typed. "Anything you want to add?" he asked, looking up.

Gregory had leaned over his shoulder to watch him work, and their faces were very close; Gregory saw Eddie's eyes dart down to his mouth, and his lips part.

"I suppose just that it's surprisingly good," Gregory heard himself say, the diplomat-politician part of his brain on autopilot while the rest of him vanished in a brief whirl of fantasy. Eddie seemed frozen, surprised perhaps. Gregory dipped his head, and Eddie's eyes closed –

And then Gregory's phone beeped, loudly.

He jerked back, setting the bowl down and digging in his pocket. He was suddenly aware he was sweaty and disheveled from his run, halfway through breakfast, and Eddie was probably just startled by how close he'd been.

"It's Alanna," he said. "She wants to know if she can move my nine-thirty to eight-thirty…"

He twisted to consult the kitchen clock; eight-ten.

"I need to shower, I need to get dressed," he said, pocketing his phone and picking up the bowl. "All right if I take this…?"

"It's your bowl," Eddie said with a grin. "Go, get ready for the day. Glad you liked it."

"Thank you, Eddie, really. And keep me posted on that brainstorming for the menus," Gregory said, and hurried out of the kitchen just as Simon was returning.

He tried to put it from his mind for most of the day, but meetings and palace business were hardly compelling enough to keep him from replaying the moment. Especially since the bowl, from which he'd eaten every scrap of the Trash Tower, sat on his desk until lunch, when palace staff replaced it with a plate of spaghetti that very clearly had Eddie's meatballs in it (they were popular in the staff kitchen too, or so he was informed). And in the afternoon his phone notified him that Eddie had posted to Photogram. Reluctantly, he set it aside for later.

Eating dinner with his father did put a damper on his thoughts, but then Eddie Rambler, curse him, was waiting in his office when he got back to it afterwards.

The chef was sitting at the window, feet propped up against the bookshelf to one side, playing a noisy game on his phone; when Gregory walked in he grinned at him and turned off the game, but he didn't get up.

"Do you know, I got Simon to try some of the Trash Tower? I told him it was better as leftovers, which is kind of a lie, but it got him to eat it," he announced, by way of greeting.

"What was the verdict?" Gregory asked, unable to resist that infectious smile.

"He told me that the only reason my ancestors weren't ashamed of me for putting mayonnaise in it was that he wouldn't consider what I'd used real mayonnaise," Eddie said. "It's potentially the most devastating burn I've ever gotten from a fellow chef, but he polished off the whole slice, so who really won?"

"Who indeed," Gregory replied, settling into his chair and spinning it to face Eddie in the window seat. He found he didn't want to ask why he was there, enjoying the friendly camaraderie of it too much.

"I put the whole conversation on Photogram, you should check it. What a hoot," Eddie declared. "I had a question for you, though."

"Fire away, you've caught the future king in an indulgent moment," Gregory told him.

"Well, I went to the royal library to do some reading this afternoon and I thought, I really don't know much about how the country sees you. Like, what public perception of the nobility is here. I think your dad was right, I do need to factor that in more, even if thinking about it doesn't mean I *use* it," Eddie said. "And so eventually I got on the internet and looked you up."

"Brave man," Gregory murmured. Eddie let his feet fall and leaned forward.

"I have to admit that one, I did not know you were gay, which normally wouldn't be relevant for a client except that you're the first out gay king of Askazer-Shivadlakia," Eddie said, tone growing serious. "And two, my immediate thought was that if I had known that, I would have come at this from a different angle, because that's a big fuckin' deal, man."

"Well, it is, and it isn't," Gregory said, mouth a little dry.

"And that was my third point," Eddie agreed. "I then thought that maybe I *shouldn't* treat it any differently, because obviously you aren't. Like no requests for, I don't know, rainbow cakes or anything."

Gregory made a face.

"Do not tell me rainbow cakes are tired or tacky, I love a rainbow cake," Eddie said, pointing at him warningly.

"No, but they're not appropriate for a coronation," Gregory said.

"Maybe. We can debate that some other time. And you know, I'm sure you don't want it to be about that, you don't want to be The Gay King, you just want to be a king," Eddie said. Gregory nodded. "Which,

I feel you, because like…I did that same math when I started my media career."

Gregory stared at him, perplexed.

"I'm bi," Eddie said. "I'm also super private about my personal life, not just that part of it, but the whole thing, so it wasn't a huge deal to me not to talk about it. But it's important in the sense of, I don't know, principles? So we had to have like…meetings about it with the network. They weren't thrilled, which is about par for the course. And I thought, okay, this doesn't have to be what I'm about right now."

"You were all right with that?" Gregory asked.

"Weren't you?"

"I came out in college," Gregory said with a shrug. "As soon as I'd sorted myself out and figured out how to…how to be me in public. But Askazer-Shivadlakia is very different from America. We don't have some of the same hangups."

"Obviously, or you wouldn't have been elected. My point is, yeah, I was okay with keeping it quiet until I could get myself established, and that's…kinda recent. So I'm not out. But I'm not like, *ashamed* of myself. That's the math I'm talking about."

He got up from the window seat, and Gregory saw what was coming with just enough clarity to know he could pull away from this if he wanted. He just…didn't want to.

So he didn't get up, not when Eddie did or when Eddie crossed to his desk, or when Eddie leaned over him, hands on the chair's armrest, face close to his once more.

"I didn't imagine you checking me out this morning," Eddie said. Gregory, slowly, shook his head. "And you haven't got anyone?"

"No."

"Mm," Eddie said thoughtfully. His eyes darted from Gregory's eyes to his lips again, then sideways, then back to his face.

"But it's unwise," Gregory said. "I can't offer much, and you're an employee – "

Eddie laughed. "I'm a contracted caterer. You're not king of my country, and I'm not particularly in the market for anything permanent."

"But I am. I need a king consort."

"Right this second?" Eddie asked. Gregory shook his head again. Eddie pulled back just a little, crouching in front of his chair, not quite so intimidating. "Then I'd like to offer you, Your Highness, a little fun while you wait for your own Prince Charming."

Gregory leaned forward and down, catching Eddie's mouth in a kiss; Eddie's hands went to his neck, thumbs on either side of his jaw.

It lasted about two seconds before Gregory overbalanced and Eddie, not in a stable position to begin with, tumbled backwards.

They ended up on the floor of his office, Eddie propped on his elbows, Gregory sprawled over him. Eddie laughed as Gregory rolled and got to his feet, reaching down to help him up. He abused the help by pulling Gregory in close and kissing him properly this time, both of them on a level. Eddie wrapped one arm around Gregory's waist.

"Lock your door and let's make out," Eddie suggested.

"I have to work here," Gregory said.

"You practically live here."

"Yes but I don't live *here*," Gregory replied impatiently. "I have an apartment with comfortable chairs and a bed and a lot more privacy."

Eddie's mouth drew up in an amused smile. "A bed, huh?"

"I'm an extremely ambitious man," Gregory told him.

"Servants won't find it weird you taking me to your apartment?" Eddie asked, but followed him when he started for the door.

"They're called staff, and they go home at night."

"Ironic," Eddie remarked, as Gregory led him into the hallway and down towards the back stairs behind the grand staircase. Gregory thought he saw someone in one of the side-hallways, but nobody emerged, so he started up the curving staircase, Eddie behind him.

"How so, ironic?" he asked, turning left at the landing and following the hallway with its row of windows that would lead them to his apartment.

"The staff get to leave, the king never does," Eddie said.

"Well, a king serves his people," Gregory replied, hoping he hadn't left his rooms messy. He couldn't think of anything particularly embarrassing that might be visible, but normally only his valet Jonas ever saw it, and Jonas was a quiet, nonjudgemental man in his sixties.

Eddie, if he even noticed such things as mess or interior decor, clearly didn't care. He followed Gregory into the sitting room, then grabbed him by one hand and beelined for the large curving sofa in front of the windows, tumbling down onto it and pulling Gregory into his lap.

From here, Gregory could look out at the sunset over the palace grounds, with the town below almost visible; he could look down at Eddie's upturned face, delighted and intent.

Or he could close his eyes and lean forward into a hell of a kiss, so he did that.

Just outside the grand staircase of the palace of Askazer-Shivadlakia, Jerry (Gerald-12th-Duke-of-Shivadlakia, he'd learned in a sing-song when he was little) intercepted disaster and, as usual, dealt with it.

Well, perhaps "as usual" was pushing it, but Jerry had a nose for drama and a knack for getting into it, so when he'd seen King Michaelis coming from one direction towards Greg's office, and Greg coming from his office with another man in tow, he gauged distances carefully and then moved to intercept.

"Uncle Mike!" he said brightly, as the king approached. "Just the man I was looking for."

"Right now, Gerald?" Michaelis asked, sounding tired. "I'm looking for Gregory."

"Already gone to bed," Jerry replied, which wasn't technically a lie. "Saw him off myself."

Michaelis got the slightly suspicious look he often got around Jerry, but Jerry supposed he deserved it. The whole family had expected him to be the responsible one, to babysit Gregory and Alanna despite only being a year older, and the whole family had been endearingly disappointed. Jerry regretted very few things in life, at least so far, and being a fellow troublemaker with those two wasn't one of them.

"I suppose it can wait until morning," Michaelis grumbled.

"Well, what's it about? Maybe I can help," Jerry said.

Michaelis looked genuinely surprised. "Help….with what?"

"Whatever you needed Gregory for. This time of night it's either a real emergency or something that should wait for morning," Jerry pointed out.

"I'm afraid it's royal business," Michaelis said, but Jerry could tell he'd successfully distracted the king from his mission. Gregory owed him one.

"In that case, it can definitely wait until morning," Jerry said with a grin. "Anyway, with all the coronation plans going off, I'm feeling extremely neglected."

Michaelis rolled his eyes, but a faint smile crossed his lips. "All right. What is it you need, Gerald?"

"I actually had a question for you. It's about farming."

That drew the king up short. "Farming? You?"

"It came up during the meeting with the Agricultural Cabinet the other day," Jerry said. "I'm becoming very interested in olives."

"Are you feeling all right?" Michaelis asked.

"I can have interests in the welfare of the country, you know," Jerry said defensively.

Michaelis, to his credit, looked apologetic. "You can, of course, and I'm sure both Gregory and I would be thrilled if you took an interest. What is it you'd like to know that you couldn't get from the Cabinet?"

"Oh, long term stuff, mostly. You know – the royal vision," Jerry said. "We don't have to talk about it now but I'd like to get on your calendar."

"Won't be my vision much longer, but Gregory and I have had some discussions…" Michaelis looked thoughtful. "I'll have a meeting arranged. You, me, and Gregory."

"Oh, ah – that'd be fine, but maybe after the coronation?" Jerry suggested.

"Why?" Michaelis asked.

Jerry rubbed his jaw. It wasn't really his business and both Gregory and his father could be stubborn about being told when they were being stupid, but after all, that was why Jerry cultivated a specific air of daffiness. People would accept a lot more advice from an idiot than an equal, for some reason.

"There's a lot on his plate," he said finally. "The coronation, taking over royal duties, briefings…maybe the unnecessary stuff can wait a little while."

"Do you think he's not up to it?" Michaelis asked. Jerry blinked.

"Uncle…nobody's up to that much," he said gently.

Michaelis seemed to consider this, which was kind of impressive.

"Is he struggling?" he asked. Jerry frowned.

"Why ask me? I barely see him these days."

"Yes, but he'd tell you things he wouldn't tell me."

That was true enough. Gregory had confided in him at school, inasmuch as he did anyone. Not for a while though, now. Jerry wondered if he confided in anyone anymore. Al might know.

"I think anyone would," he finally said, diplomatically. "I'm sure if he starts to really drown he'll speak up, but Gregory's idea of drowning and our idea…" he made a weighing motion. He hadn't meant to get quite this deep just to keep Michaelis from walking in on his son with a secret lover, but, well, carpe diem.

"It's a good point," Michaelis said, eyes going distant. "Very good point. Well. Thank you, Jerry. Speak to Alanna about setting up that meeting whenever you think is best. But I'm going to hold you to that interest in olives," he added, shaking a finger at him.

"Absolutely," Jerry promised. "Goodnight, uncle."

"Goodnight, Gerald," Michaelis said, and went back the way he'd come, towards his own apartments in a different wing of the palace. Jerry, deciding this was enough hard work for the week, slumped onto the grand staircase, resting his head against the post of the banister.

"Deftly done," said a new voice, and Alanna stepped out from the shadows. Jerry, startled, clutched his chest.

"You could have helped," he said, scowling as she sat next to him.

"And ruin the moment? You did fine. Though I should warn you, if you keep behaving competently, they'll keep giving you work."

"I could take an interest in things," Jerry protested. "I might be turning over a new leaf, for all you know."

"Well, you did Gregory a favor, anyway, so I suppose I should thank you. What was all that about?" Alanna asked.

Jerry shrugged. "When did you come in?"

"Just as you buttonholed His Majesty."

"Ah. Well, you didn't hear it from me," Jerry said, tapping the side of his nose. "I was preventing trouble. Himself was coming down the hall looking for Greg just as Greg was taking an *amore* up to his rooms."

Alanna blinked at him. "An *amore*?"

"Boyfriend? Or at least, a date. I didn't get a good look but it was definitely an assignation."

"He isn't even dating anyone right now," Alanna said. "That was the whole point of the arranged marriage discussion."

"Well, he's clearly doing some arranging," Jerry replied. Alanna still looked unsettled. "He's a big boy, Al, I'm sure he's fine."

"It's not that I'm worried about," she said. "All this stress…he's not himself."

"I don't know. I don't see him as much as you, but seems like the best stress relief possible just followed him up the stairs."

"Creep," she said affectionately. "Thanks for covering, though."

"All part of the royal service. I am interested, you know."

"In Greg's *amore?*"

"No, sorry, back a few changes of subject," Jerry said. "In the olives. When I was talking with Uncle Mike. The agricultural meeting got me thinking. I didn't know crop planning was such a precise science."

"Precision hasn't usually been one of your strong suits," Alanna pointed out.

"No, but I love all that kind of planning stuff. Timetables. Like those word puzzles they used to give us in school."

Alanna twisted a little, resting her chin on his shoulder. "Well, well. Everyone's growing up at last."

"Slander," Jerry said.

"Maybe, but I'm giving you a new job," Alanna said.

"I didn't have an old one."

"Fine, I'm giving you a first job," she said. "His Majesty listens to you because he knows you have no political agenda, which is a belief you can only weaponize for a short time. From now until the coronation, your job is to run interference on the king. Get him to leave Greg alone as much as possible outside of meetings. And if this *amore* hangs around, keep him out of the king's way."

Jerry looked down at her, eyes wide. "Keeping the prince away from the king?" he asked. Then, delighted, "Am I the evil vizier?"

"If you do a good job I will have Gregory officially appoint you vizier when he's king," she said.

"We haven't had a vizier in a hundred years," Jerry said, pretending to be star-struck. "What would I even do?"

"Nothing," Alanna said, "but with great drama."

"Sold," Jerry replied, and kissed her temple. "Go to bed. I'm headed there and Gregory's clearly already gone."

"Fair enough. If you find out who the *amore* is, let me know," she said, standing and dusting the seat of her trousers. Jerry gave her a thumbs up, then leaned back on the stairs to watch her go.

Eddie left the royal chambers (as he called them, narrating the adventure silently to himself) around midnight, well-satisfied with the world. He didn't expect to run into anyone, but he wasn't truly at ease until he'd made it back down to ground level and through the main hallway to the guest wing.

Eddie came from a family of people for whom the world held endless possibility, and he was rarely surprised when his unorthodox life brought him to new adventures. Still, this was high on the "didn't predict that" scale. After a couple of seasons of success on television he hadn't really blinked at being hired to cater a coronation, but there was still a certain spice in going halfway around the world to make out with the soon-to-be king of a delightful little coastal city-state.

In private, away from his office and staff, Gregory was different. He'd seen a little of it in their walk to town, and their morning meeting in the garden, and – really almost anytime he was in Simon's kitchen or in Eddie's company without others around. The tension in his body dissipated, and his face became startlingly expressive. As he unlocked the door to his own suite, Eddie beamed to himself over Gregory's dark eyelashes and half-open mouth from a few minutes before.

It couldn't be easy to be one of the few visibly gay royals on the continent (in the world? Eddie didn't pay much attention to royalty, usually) but Gregory had apparently been very intentional about it, and he went about enjoying himself the same way, without the least hint of shame. If, perhaps, a little exaggerated dignity.

Well, at least they'd gotten past him calling Eddie "Mr. Dude."

Very well past.

Eddie settled cross-legged on the foot of his bed, checking his appearance in the selfie-camera view on his phone before hitting record.

"Evening, friends and fans," he said, keeping his voice low. "I'm pretty sure it's like lunchtime where most of you are, but I'm keeping quiet because it's late here. Just thought I'd say a happy goodnight to everyone – every day here brings new challenges but also new delights. And at the end of the day I'm always ready to sleep. Even if it's just so I can get up tomorrow and try again."

He gave them his goofiest smile, wondering if Gregory watched these videos. "So I'll say goodnight to you locals here in Askazer-Shivadlakia, and I hope everyone in America's having a wonderful afternoon, and…well, good morning to Japan, I guess."

He put up the peace sign, tilting his head towards it. "Everybody eat at least one really good meal today, okay? Night, you all."

FOUR WEEKS UNTIL
THE CORONATION OF HIS MAJESTY
KING GREGORY III

GREGORY WOKE, THE morning after his evening with Eddie, feeling energized and cheerful. It didn't immediately occur to him why, until he spotted his shirt, lying across the sofa where Eddie had tossed it last night. Gregory had tried to catch it, to set it aside in a more orderly kind of way, and Eddie had laughed and distracted him.

"Not everything's gotta be filed," Eddie had said, and the sentiment had struck a chord he hadn't really examined at the time. Now, looking back, the reminder that sometimes you had to simply let a mess be a mess had felt very freeing. The whole world didn't have to be in order before he could be crowned.

Pleased at the idea, he took a little longer in the shower than usual, and Jonas had come and gone with his clothes, whisking away the messy shirt and leaving clean ones. Gregory dressed, deciding on a bright blue shirt from the two the valet had left, and met Alanna in the hall on the way to breakfast.

"Good morning," he said, wondering if Eddie might be pestering Simon in the kitchen. "Sleep well?"

"I did, thank you," she replied, flipping her hair over her shoulder. "You look nice."

"Thank you. Begin as you mean to go on, I guess," he told her. "Not to trumpet the perks of being king, but it's easier when you have staff who pick out your clothes. What's my first meeting this morning?"

"The usual briefing, but otherwise you're open until about two. Because of the – "

"Budget meeting that I need to do the numbers on," he agreed, peeking into the kitchen. Just Simon, frying eggs.

"Good morning, Your Highness," Simon said.

"Morning," Gregory replied. He held up three fingers to indicate how many eggs he wanted and Simon nodded. As they headed to the dining room, Gregory caught Alanna smiling at him in a way that made him suspicious, but he couldn't put his finger on why.

Michaelis was at breakfast, eating toast and reading something on a tablet; to Gregory's surprise, Jerry was also up and working his way through an omelet. Alanna took a scone from the dish and settled in, spreading it with jam.

"Good morning, Gregory," Michaelis said, looking up briefly from his tablet. "You look well rested. Bed early last night?"

"And some good sleep," Gregory agreed. Jerry made a soft noise, but when Gregory looked over all he saw was an innocent smile.

"Just as well. Have you got a few minutes this morning?" Michaelis asked. A look crossed Jerry's face that Michaelis seemed to register. "I'll try to keep it brief," he added.

"Sure, after the staff meeting. Al – "

"Adding it to your calendar," she agreed, tapping on her phone.

"You should go to bed early more often. You're in high spirits today," Michaelis said, somewhere between approval and a grumble. The others bit their lips. Gregory wasn't sure what was going on, but it looked like Al and Jerry might be conspiring. Given one was his assistant and both were family, it'd probably be to his benefit to stay ignorant.

"I'll bear that in mind," he said, as Simon came in with the eggs and more toast. "I didn't see Eddie in there with you this morning, Simon."

"Ah, no," Simon agreed. "I think he's spending much of the day with the Conservation officers. He seems very determined on the subject of wild boar."

"Hear there's good eating on those. Acorns all winter and berries all summer, makes them tender," Michaelis remarked. "The nonkosher butcher pays top dollar. Devil to hunt, though."

"Alanna," Gregory said, considering things, "Could you block off the hour before the budget meeting today? Just mark it busy on the calendar."

"Sure. Anyone to add to the meeting?"

"No, I want to have time to clear my head beforehand. If anyone has issues today, they'll know to come to me before one."

"Shall I hold lunch, Your Highness?" Simon asked.

"No, I'll be going out," Gregory said. Simon's eyebrows rose. "Actually, can you pack a lunch? On the large side. I'll take it with me."

"Of course," Simon replied, as Alanna set the meeting in the calendar. "It will be ready in the kitchen at one."

Not everything had to be filed, and Eddie had been clear he was here for a good time. Gregory could make a little mess in at least one corner of his life, for now.

The palace of Askazer-Shivadlakia was technically public property. The grounds, including the lake, fishing lodge, trails, and a portion of the forest, were administered and cared for by the conservation corps, which Gregory's grandfather had founded. Because of this, there was a visitor's center not far from the palace, and that had to be where Eddie had taken his bowfishing lessons. It was probably where he was trying to convince some poor conservation officer to let him hunt a wild boar.

Gregory hummed to himself as he made his way down the trail to the visitor's center, the small basket of food swinging from one hand. Not only was he getting a well-needed breath of fresh air before an all-afternoon meeting, but he'd have a good lunch by the lake with Eddie.

Besides, Eddie probably hadn't packed a lunch, and it was a nice gesture. Although…

He stopped outside the low fence of the visitor's center. Eddie had been very casual about this – they both had – and bringing him a picnic lunch after they'd spent the previous evening on the couch together…

"Your Highness!" Eddie's voice rang out from the left, and Gregory turned to see him, two conservation officers, and (unsettlingly) a man with a guitar, all loitering on the rocks at the edge of the lake's beach. "Come over, we're all down here."

"So I see," Gregory replied, steeling himself for an awkward moment. "Have you found a folk song about the wild boar yet?"

"How'd you know?" Eddie asked, laughing.

"I saw the guitar," Gregory said. The man with the guitar smiled at him respectfully.

"What brings you out here?" Eddie asked.

"Oh, I ah…" Gregory held up the basket. "I wanted a break from work, and imagined you hadn't brought a lunch with you."

Eddie beamed at him. "From Simon?"

"Well, I definitely didn't make it," Gregory said, passing the basket over. The conservation officers gave him a nod as they left, and the man with the guitar high-fived Eddie and walked off down the beach. Eddie began unpacking the basket onto a flat rock, gesturing for Gregory to take the slightly more sloped rock next to it.

"Join me, Simon packed more food than even I can eat," he said, laying out bread and cheese, a little jar of mustard and a pot of olive oil, some dried figs. "Productive morning, I hope?"

"Yes, very. Not as interesting as yours, I imagine," Gregory said.

"Well, I definitely learned a lot," Eddie agreed.

He looked up in time to catch Gregory watching him, and Gregory smiled. Eddie matched it, and then they were both laughing quietly.

"This was very sweet of you," Eddie said.

"Not a little over the top?" Gregory asked.

"No, why would it be? Got you out of that stuffy office, and tells me you wanted to see me."

"I wouldn't want to be obvious."

"Why not? I would," Eddie replied. "I like being obvious. Means nobody ever doubts where you stand. Why wouldn't you want to spend time with me? I'm delightful. I definitely didn't expect I'd get to see you today, or at least not so soon, and that's great."

Gregory considered this. There was a charm to being obvious, he supposed, especially if you were as charismatic as Eddie. It was refreshing, to say the least.

"Well, then I'm glad I came down," he replied.

"Me too. Now, let's eat," Eddie pronounced, and Gregory nodded and bent to his food. "You listen attentively while I tell you the legends of your people I have just now learned from a park ranger."

Later that evening he was glad he'd taken a break; the budget meeting, infuriatingly but also expectedly, ran long. Staff brought in dinner during the course of it, and by the time he'd finally handshaked-

and-armclapped the last of the attendees out the door, it was late.

He considered going in search of Eddie, even stopping by his suite, but decided against it. Eddie was a perceptive man; he'd have seen that Gregory was in a meeting and found some other entertainment.

When he reached the door of his apartments, there was a neon pink sticky-note on the handle that read "DO NOT DISTURB" in Eddie's sprawling hand.

Gregory grinned, plucked it off the knob, and tucked it in a pocket as he stepped inside.

The light was on in his bedroom, and he could see one of Eddie's loud-print shirts against the bedspread. When he leaned in the doorway, he could see the rest of Eddie as well – still in his clothes, loud shirt included, but sprawled on top of the bed, asleep, one hand on his chest and the other above his head.

He had a post-it note stuck to his forehead that said, "Disturb".

Gregory plucked it up and laughed; Eddie startled awake, and then tilted his head against the pillow.

"Hey, thank you for disturbing," Eddie said, smiling warmly.

"One does one's best. You didn't need to wait up," Gregory said.

"Good, because I clearly didn't. What time is it?"

"Only about ten."

"Power nap, then," Eddie said, sitting up and crossing his legs. "I thought you might want a friendly ear after the late meeting. Or a friendly hand," he added, waggling his eyebrows. Gregory sat on the edge of the bed next to him and then flopped back, stretching. Eddie rested a palm on his stomach.

"Listen, I will not be hurt if you are tired and want me to fuck off," Eddie said. "Just so we're clear."

"Not at all, I'm glad you're here. But I'm not sure I'm the most inspired person right now, given I've still got the words 'fiscal year' imprinted on my eyelids," Gregory replied. "Just so your expectations are correct."

"No expectations here," Eddie said. "If you want me to stay – "

"I do."

"Well, good," Eddie answered. He leaned over, filling Gregory's vision, and kissed him. "Want a truly wild suggestion?" he asked, against Gregory's mouth.

"I'm learning the folly of saying yes to you," Gregory said.

"How about you go to bed and I will also go to bed, but in this bed, and we can continue the conversation when we wake up?"

Gregory could feel the moment his muscles relaxed, the drop from King Ascendant to Crown Prince all the way down to just Gregory.

"That sounds amazing," he said.

"I know!" Eddie sat back and reached out, pulling him upright. "Go get changed."

Roughly eight minutes later, in a worn old shirt and cotton shorts, Gregory shuffled under the covers and felt Eddie climb in behind him, wrapping around his body like a large, sleepy bear. He closed his eyes and let himself go blissfully slack.

"I've never said this to anyone before," Eddie said, as Gregory drifted off, "But I'm going to enjoy the hell out of sleeping next to you."

The next morning, when he woke up and Eddie was indeed still in the bed – sprawled out over Gregory's chest, gently snoring into his collarbone – Gregory managed to find his fast-dying phone in the bedclothes and text Jonas not to come in until summoned. Eddie mumbled sleepily into his chest.

"Time 'sit?" he asked.

"Early yet. Just letting my valet know not to interrupt us," Gregory replied, patting Eddie's pale hair, sticking out wildly from his head. "Sleep a little longer if you'd care to."

"No, I'm up," Eddie decided, pushing away just enough so that he could roll over onto his side. Gregory plugged the phone into its charger and then turned to face him, curious. "Sleep well?"

"I did, yes."

"Good. Al worries you don't sleep enough."

"Ah, Al to you too now, is it?" Gregory asked, amused.

"She's great. And she cares a lot about you."

"I know. I care for her, too. It's not often the noble families have children who get along. Lots of attempted murders between cousins in past generations."

"Huh." Eddie rolled onto his back, looking up at the ceiling. "Must be weird, having roots that deep. Like, how far back can you go in the family tree?"

"Not terribly far on my father's side – two, three generations past him, when they arrived in the country. My mother was old nobility, I can probably get back fifteen generations on her side. But yes…there's a strong foundation of history to stand on. Thank goodness, all things considered. You sound like you're close to your family. Surely you understand what that's like."

"A little." Eddie shrugged. "It's really just my parents, though. My mom's parents are big hippies, they've been in a couple of cults, and we're not actually sure where they are at any given moment. They've got a VW Bus and a will to wander."

"My goodness."

"Good people but not like…dependable. And Dad's parents don't like him so they don't see us much."

"Whyever not?" Gregory asked.

"They're real Stepford types. They don't acknowledge I exist."

"Because you're a TV chef?"

"Among other things. The shame and horror," Eddie said, grinning. "Dad and I don't like them either so it's no big deal. They think I'm trashy, that's all. Lots of people do."

Gregory thought reservedly of his objections when Alanna had hired Eddie. *I wanted gastropub, not dive bar.* Eddie laughed, and Gregory realized it must have shown on his face.

"Yeah, that's about the size of it," Eddie said, though Gregory hadn't even spoken. "Look, I do a show about working-class food and the working-class people who make it. Restaurants that I put on the show get huge bumps in business. If I like the food, I invest as a silent partner. I've got a portfolio of dive bars and greasy spoons from Bangor to Baja. Hell, after the coronation I'm going to drop a few grand in Askazer-Shivadlakia, too. Luxury cheese exports and handicrafts. My folks raised me to believe in what I do. Other people don't have to."

"A very healthy way to live, I suppose."

"It has its pain in the ass moments, but I do love it. There's real freedom in not giving a damn. Sooner or later I'm going to get tired of television, being on the road all the time, and I like knowing my whole identity isn't tied up in it. I can walk away if I ever want to."

"No firm ideas for the future?"

Eddie shrugged against the sheets. "How do you make fate laugh?"

"Announce your plans," Gregory said. "We've heard that one in Askazer-Shivadlakia."

"Which reminds me, realistically, this week we need to set the theme and menu for the banquet."

Gregory groaned, covering his face with his hands. Eddie rolled, propping himself up, and kissed the backs of Gregory's hands.

"Don't worry. I'll pull something off, I always do. You have a good kitchen staff, they'll help, and I'm going to try to source all the food locally, so we won't need to worry about shipping delays."

"If we can't come up with something that Dad likes, I think we should just go with the formal meal," Gregory said.

"You're the boss. It's not interesting, but it is safe. I'll have Alanna set a final tasting for the end of the week, we'll make sure your dad's in a good mood, and I'll do my best to knock his socks off. In the meantime," Eddie added, pulling one of Gregory's hands away from his face, "I should shower and sneak out before anyone's up. Wanna come shower with me?"

That was the week guests began trickling in for the coronation. Not many at first, since there was a full month until coronation, but distant family began returning for a nice long holiday on the coast, and a handful of reporters started to set up shop and look around for local color. Gregory began to be interrupted with requests for interviews, local television spots, and occasionally a royal favor for a family friend.

He was running late for a call-in to a podcast recording, and was literally running from the conference room to his office, when he burst into the main hall and almost bowled over a crowd of elderly women. He skidded to a stop, startled, and as one they turned to look at him with interested eyes.

"Your Highness!" Eddie called, from the middle of the knot of women, at least a head taller than any of them. "Everybody curtsey!"

Gregory stared, mortified, as two dozen women, all visibly over the age of sixty, dropped into dainty curtseys they'd clearly learned in school as children. Without even meaning to, he fell into tradition as well, stiffly bowing at the waist, deep enough to demonstrate his respect for their age. A few laughed.

"All right, nonnas, come on, this way," Eddie continued, leading the women towards the big staff-canteen kitchen. "Show a little of that Shivadh hustle!"

He wanted to stop and find out what was going on, because it certainly looked interesting, but his phone beeped insistently. He put it from his mind as he ducked into his office, where Alanna had already set up a mic for recording. It wasn't until that evening, eating dinner in the family dining room, that he remembered what he'd seen.

"Did you happen to see the gaggle of grannies in the castle today?" he asked Alanna over a bowl of pasta – an old highland recipe with thick noodles and seared, thin-sliced beef.

"Oh yeah! Eddie had them in to give him a demo. You're eating the result," she said, pointing her fork at his bowl. He looked down, surprised. "He wanted lessons in hand-pulled noodles and what we do with them around here. He rounded up every woman in town who still makes her own and threw a party."

"A noodle-pulling party?"

"Can't argue with results," she said. "He's got kids coming in tomorrow to help him learn how to make cookies. Don't worry, I got releases signed by the parents and there are plenty of chaperones."

"Doubt that's going to help with the coronation feast."

Alanna looked complacent about it. "You never know. Anyway," she added, studying her phone, "You can take some of that to-go if you want, you don't have anything booked for this evening."

He frowned. "Why would I want to take some to go?"

"I don't know. If you wanted some later, or to share with someone," she said airily.

Gregory stared at her, setting his fork down. "Who would I be meeting that you didn't know about?"

Alanna gave him a look. Gregory felt his eyes widen.

"I don't know who he is and I don't need to – " she began, but he cut her off with a gesture.

"It's not serious," he said. "I mean – it's not a relationship, not really. It's just some fun. I had thought we were being discreet."

"Like I said. Don't know who he is," Alanna said. "Frankly, I think it's good for you."

"Is this what you and Jerry were giggling about at breakfast the other day?" he demanded.

"Yes," she said unrepentantly.

"Does Dad know?"

"If he does, it's not from me or Jerry. But no, I don't think so."

"Well, small mercy."

"Why?" she asked. "I'm sure he'd be thrilled. Isn't this what he – ah," she said, as Gregory pointed at her.

"A little too thrilled. And he's not a candidate, anyhow," Greg said.

"That's a cruel thing to say about a date." Alanna looked appalled.

"He's not interested in long-term, is what I mean. And even if he were he wouldn't…" Gregory searched for the word. "I don't know that he'd enjoy the royal life."

"Well, as long as you're having fun," she said.

Gregory considered this. "You know, I think I am."

"Good." She gathered up her phone, standing. "I'll see you tomorrow morning – yell if you need anything."

"Alanna," he called, as she reached the doorway. She turned. "You know if there was someone serious I'd tell you. I value your opinion tremendously."

She grinned. "You'd better. Until tomorrow, Your Highness."

Eddie, still dotted here and there with flour and hugely pleased with himself over the noodle lesson, was helping scrub down the big kitchen that fed most of the palace staff when someone walked in and said, "You!" loudly at him.

"Indeed, it is I," he replied, bowing low and flicking a tea towel off his shoulder in a salute. When he straightened, a man with a faint resemblance to the royal family was staring at him. "I'm afraid I haven't read my Who's Who, but you're probably one of the noble cousins, huh?" Eddie asked, grinning.

The man dodged someone going past with a pile of dirty plates and hustled into the kitchen, squinting at him.

"You're Eddie Rambler," he said, surprised.

"Most of the time," Eddie agreed, offering one slightly damp, soapy hand, then wiping it with a towel before re-offering it.

"Oh! Sorry, I'm Jerry," the man said, taking his hand. "Gerald, Duke of Shivadlakia."

"You're the bad example!" Eddie said, delighted.

Jerry laughed. "Is that how Greg described me?"

"It's how everyone describes you," Eddie said. "They also always add they think I'll like you, which is either a statement about me or a testament to your likability."

"Probably both," Jerry said. "Sorry, about three separate facts are coming together in my head and I'm still sorting them out. You're here to cater the coronation."

"Yep," Eddie agreed, going back to wiping down the steel prep counter.

"It's only the last time I saw you I didn't realize you were, well, you," Jerry said. "I'd have introduced myself before now if I'd known. Offered to show you around, sort of thing."

"Wouldn't say no now," Eddie replied, wondering where Jerry had seen him earlier. "Well, actually, I would, but only for tonight. If you're into giving tours I'll take a ticket for tomorrow."

"Honestly, I wouldn't know where to begin. And I'm sure you've been kept very busy," Jerry remarked. "How's preparations coming?"

"It's a work in progress," Eddie replied. "Hey, I've been asking everyone today, what's your favorite food?"

"Cocktails," Jerry replied.

"Huh. Actually, that might be helpful," Eddie said thoughtfully. "I'm considering a kind of country house murder mystery vibe, given everyone's going to be in tuxes and gowns anyway."

"I'm being fitted for my gown tomorrow," Jerry said.

"I'm sure you'll wear the hell out of it."

Jerry laughed. "I see why Greg likes you. And a little bit why Al says Uncle Michaelis is..."

"Of no strong opinion?" Eddie asked drily. "Yeah. He might go for the cocktails thing, though, as long as I don't actually present it as *country house murder mystery*."

"Murder vibes not appropriate for a coronation?" Jerry suggested.

"I think it's fine, but you can see the problem he might have. Anyway, he wants a formal dinner. If I can pull him in with swanky custom cocktails, he might be more open to innovation in the food." Eddie gave the table a final swipe, then turned back to Jerry. "Thank you, Your Grace."

"My, you've been reading the comportment books! Jerry's fine. I don't stand on ceremony." Jerry clapped him on the shoulder. "Keep up the good work."

"Keepin' it new," Eddie said, and Jerry laughed as he walked off.

"Psst – hey!"

Gregory, leaning back in his chair with his boots up on his desk and phone in hand, looked up from a muted Photogram video. The video showing Eddie making cookies with children – including what looked like some of the younger noble cousins – and when he looked away it was to find a real-life Eddie leaning in the window of his office, arms resting on the sill.

"I was just catching up on your extremely busy day," Gregory said, pointing at his phone. Eddie grinned.

"So you know that I have cookies to share," Eddie replied.

"I have a feeling we'll be eating cookies until my diamond jubilee."

"Do you get one of those if you're elected? I guess nobody's going to say you can't have one. Anyway I have a bag of cookies," Eddie said, holding up a bag in one hand, "and also a bag of wine," he added, indicating a slim backpack on his back.

"Sounds like you're on your way to a grand adventure," Gregory remarked.

"Come along. I'm going to hide out in the gardens and watch the stars come out."

Technically, he shouldn't; he had to finish this speech soon to get it to the communications people tomorrow to be doctored up and returned to him so he could give it at the opening of the royal vault so they could get the crown jewels out.

So that he could be crowned with them, which still felt surreal.

On the other hand, he could blow the speech off, at least for a little while; it was bound to be relaxing, and he'd had a full day.

Eddie cheered when Gregory dropped his boots to the floor and got up, coming to kneel at the window bench and look down at him.

"What kind of wine?" he asked.

"Why, are you picky?" Eddie retorted.

"I want to know my coronation banquet chef is pairing wine with cookies properly."

"Not intentionally, I just stole what I saw. It's a Riesling, that's a dessert wine! It'll be fine."

Gregory nodded and slid around, dangling his legs out the window; Eddie stepped back and he dropped down, grateful for Eddie's steadying hands.

"Here," Eddie said, offering him a bar of shortbread. "For the journey."

"How many cookies have you already eaten today?" Gregory asked, nibbling on it while they walked.

"Not that many. I learned how to eat for an audience years ago," Eddie said, clearly leading the way to some goal he had on the palace grounds. "The rule is that you never take more than one bite for the camera. You watch any food television host. They take one bite of everything. The rest is a camera cut that leaves the meal to your imagination. It's part of why food shows make people hungry."

"That's a good trick."

"Small bites and big reactions," Eddie said. "Key to what I do."

"It's not far off how one gets a law passed around here, either," Gregory replied. "It's good shortbread."

"Potato starch," Eddie said.

"Oh yes?"

"Probably doesn't help with law making, but it's great in shortbread." Eddie ducked through a gap in a high hedge and led him into a little clearing that looked down on the harbor. From this angle the town was almost across the water from them, lights slowly going on in shops and houses. They'd barely penetrate the darkness once the sun was fully down.

The backpack Eddie brought had two bottles of wine wrapped in a blanket; he set the bottles aside and shook out the blanket, spreading it on the ground before opening the first bottle with a corkscrew on a pocket-knife. Gregory settled himself on the blanket and leaned against his shoulder, watching him pour.

"We have a bouquet of cookies for you this evening, some of which may even make it into the coronation menu," Eddie said, handing him a glass of wine. He opened the other bag and revealed a covered bowl stocked with various sweets. "The only ones not included are the tricolors, because those take like two days to make."

"I've had tricolors. Very fond of them, actually."

"Duly noted," Eddie replied. "I'm tempted to veer away from anything with nuts for the official event, but there are these, which are walnutty things, and these almond whatses, and some of the chocolate chip cookies have pecans in them."

"Yes, the very famously traditional Shivadh chocolate chip cookies," Gregory drawled.

"Chocolate chip cookies have been around since the 1930s. Almost a hundred years. I actually had a look in some of the previous chefs' personal cookbooks in the library, you know when chocolate chip cookies made it here?"

"I couldn't begin to guess."

"Me either. The notes don't say. But chocolate chips made it here in 1946. There's records of chefs using them instead of full bars of chocolate because you could get the chips but not the bars. Some kind of rationing issue. Anyway," Eddie said, "your granddad ate chocolate chip cookies in this palace, that's good enough tradition for me."

"Then me too, I suppose," Gregory said, taking one.

"Wanna eat it like a food host?" Eddie asked. Gregory gestured for him to continue. Eddie held up a cookie, broke off a chunk about the size of a coin, and popped it into his mouth. He rolled his eyes, groaned in appreciation, and waved the hand not holding his wine glass dramatically. "Now you."

"I'm not going to groan like that," Gregory warned, but he did break off a chunk like he'd seen Eddie do, and when he ate it he couldn't help but nod in appreciation.

"All that dignity's going to catch up with you one day," Eddie said.

"Probably already has. Too late to do anything about it now," Gregory said. He began picking at the other cookies, trying a little of each, while Eddie explained what each was and told stories about the kids who'd brought the recipes. By the time he'd sampled everything, the first bottle of wine was empty, and they were both lying back on the blanket, staring upwards, Eddie giving a sort of impromptu lesson in the history of the cookie.

"I thought you studied theatre in school," he said, as Eddie paused in his discussion of the uses of date honey in early recipes for baklava. "And somewhere in there you must have learned to cook. When did you have time for history as well?"

"I had a lot of backstage time during rehearsal and access to a good library," Eddie answered. "I like history. Might go back and get a degree in it someday."

"You don't think it would be strange? Going back to school as Eddie Rambler?"

"Sure. Strange as attending college as Prince Gregory ben Michaelis to begin with," Eddie answered.

"I suppose that's a point." Gregory rolled over, propping himself on his elbows. Eddie gazed up at him serenely. "You could put out a line of dormitory cookware."

"Don't think it hasn't crossed my mind. Always thinking, me," Eddie said. "That reminds me, I've got a question for you. I've been asking everyone lately, just to see what they say."

"Of course."

"When you were a kid, what was your favorite food?"

"Hm." Gregory thought about it, plucking at the grass just at the edge of the blanket. "You'd think it would be something unique – something only served in Askazer-Shivadlakia."

"Like what?"

"Oh, I don't know. Kuzhui, perhaps."

"Kuz what now?"

Gregory smiled at him. "Kuzhui. It's a kind of casserole made with flaked fish."

"That certainly sounds unique."

"But when I went off to boarding school, eating in the dining hall every day…" Gregory shrugged. "It was good food, but it was meant to feed a lot of growing children very quickly. And school wasn't nearby, so the food was different, too. I did miss Simon's cooking."

"What did he make that was so good?"

"Not the fish casserole," Gregory said. Eddie chuckled. "No, what I really wanted that first holiday home from school was potato salad."

"Potato salad!"

"Sure. It was a very specific cold potato salad my mother used to pack in a thermos, for when we went to the fishing lodge. That first day, we'd get there just before sunset. My father would bowfish, and my mother and I sat in the boat and ate potato salad on crackers, and read books. At least until I was fourteen or so, and Dad started teaching me to bowfish too."

"That sounds nice, actually," Eddie said. "Simon's recipe?"

"My mother taught him to make it. She learned from her family chef. We still have it once in a while, but usually only at the fishing lodge. We don't go boating as often anymore. What about you?" he asked, aware he was rambling back into nostalgia.

"Oh, I don't go boating much either," Eddie said. Gregory nudged him with an elbow. "Well, I do make a decent potato salad."

"But what was your favorite food?"

Eddie tucked his arms behind his head, closing his eyes. "It's a little gross."

"Fish casserole," Gregory reminded him.

"Well, also the food isn't material, it was part of something bigger. Kind of like how yours is, actually. On weekends or whenever we could weasel out of school, my folks would throw us in the car and take us on day trips or overnights to, I don't know, wherever – national parks, tourist traps, different beaches with cool waves for surfing. Plenty to see in California if you drive pretty much any direction from the coast. We'd get up super early, pack the car with games to keep us busy and coolers full of lunch, and hit the road. Eventually we'd stop off somewhere and eat lunch at a picnic table or on the beach or whatever. It was the travel that made it special."

"What was in the lunches?"

"Chips, for sure. Celery sticks, peanut butter. Cheese and crackers – real cheap cheese, bless my parents. Bananas. Soda and juice. And we all made our own sandwiches so we'd have what we liked, then we'd wrap them in waxed paper and put them in the very top of the cooler, so they'd stay cold but they wouldn't get soggy."

"Very rustic," Gregory remarked.

"That's a charming word for it. Anyway, a sandwich eaten out of a waxed paper wrapper, that was my best meal."

"Any kind of sandwich?"

Eddie opened his eyes, amused. "I had a specialty. Peanut butter, banana, and bacon bits, with hot sauce."

Gregory knew he couldn't keep the look off his face, so didn't try. Eddie pointed at him, snickering.

"That's what my siblings looked like. Kept them from trying to steal my sandwich, though."

"It'd keep me from trying, certainly."

"Don't knock it. Although probably all the fresh air and getting to skip school contributed to the flavor." Eddie sat up, stretching a little. "There's a lot here that reminds me of home. It's that balmy warm weather in the evenings, especially. Really beautiful nights you have in this burg."

"We put them on specially for visitors."

"As long as it doesn't rain, your coronation's probably going to have gorgeous weather."

"I hope so. I won't see much of it. Trapped inside most of the day making oaths and wearing extremely heavy hats and robes."

"Huh," Eddie said, in a way that made Gregory look up at him. "That is a shame. You and your dad are both pretty outdoorsy, right?"

"I suppose so. A little less now that he's older, but yes."

"And everyone loves a picnic," Eddie said thoughtfully. Gregory sat up too, watching him.

"What are you thinking?" he asked.

"Well, picture this," Eddie said. "Coronation's over. Everyone's leaving the, what, the throne room?"

"Yes."

"Stuffy in there?"

"Extremely."

"Late afternoon. We're all ready for a drink and something to eat. Everyone's in a good mood because their very handsome and charismatic new king has been crowned."

"Thank you," Gregory said.

"Welcome. As they leave the throne room, they're guided outside into the palace gardens – "

"Charming, but we can't make diplomats sit on blankets," Gregory said, catching his drift.

"No, I wasn't going to. I was thinking cafe tables, like they have at the bistros in town. Draped in checked tablecloth, in the kingdom's colors. Lawn chairs with cushions. Not formal, but very well presented. And on every table there's a picnic basket."

"Like a gift," Gregory said, enthralled by the idea.

"The baskets have a bottle of wine, little jars of mustard, jam, honey – people love stuff in little jars," Eddie said. "Snack foods. Cookies to eat with the big cake Simon can bring out at the end of the meal."

"But what's the meal itself?"

"In the basket, finger sandwiches in waxed paper – maybe beeswax wrap, that's more environmentally sound. Fresh whole fruit. But that's just the foundation. Here's the spectacle," Eddie said, turning fully to him. "Just as everyone sits down, waiters come out of the palace with thermoses. Two for each table. Hot soup in one, cold potato salad in the other. Your mother's recipe. To honor her. What kind of soup does your dad like?"

"There's a mushroom soup – "

"Perfect. Hot soup, cold potato salad, sandwiches, snacks, fruit, wine. Easy to prep – time intensive but not difficult to make. Easy to get everything I need, too."

"I like it," Gregory said. "I like the idea of – being king at that banquet."

"Will your dad go for it?"

"Maybe. Probably. If we make the presentation formal enough."

Eddie grinned. "We, huh? Well, let me come up with a sales pitch for him."

"How?"

"Not sure yet, but I'll figure it out. This time the presentation will be more for him than for you anyway. I can think about that later. I'll give it to him this weekend, that'll give me a few days to pretty everything up."

Gregory saw real pleasure and interest in Eddie's eyes, which were lit up with the idea. He leaned in and kissed him, feeling oddly as though he could capture a little of that euphoria.

Eddie made a soft noise and grabbed the front of his shirt, deepening the kiss. Gregory figured this one was on Eddie to write down and file away and work on, so he let himself be distracted for a while.

Eddie held up his phone, camera aimed outward for once, and called, "Simon! Simon, turn around."

Simon, standing over a pan at the stove, announced, "*Je refuse!*"

"Aw, come on Simon!"

"I will not be held hostage to a telephone," Simon continued, sounding as even-toned as ever.

"You're the hottest new food media star, though," Eddie pleaded, circling to one side. "Give them all a look at your beautiful face!"

He caught just the edge of Simon's eyeroll, which was enough encouragement for him.

"I am not a performing internet monkey," Simon said, but he did give the camera a dry look.

"Hah, looking good. So tell us what you're doing," Eddie said, aiming the camera down into the pot.

"I am checking the doneness on the potatoes," Simon told him. "For potato salad."

"And why potato salad?"

"Because you have a harebrained scheme," Simon announced.

Eddie turned himself and also the phone, so that he could capture Simon in a shot with him. "It's true. All my schemes are like this," he told the camera. "But you like me anyway, huh?"

"You're charming, so I forgive you," Simon said, shaking a finger at him.

"I'll take it. What goes into the potato salad?"

"Palace secret. But I can tell you that you must include cider vinegar and garlic. And of course it helps if your personal paid chef made it for you."

Eddie laughed. "Personal paid *celebrity* chef. My followers made you a fan club. They've got t-shirts and everything."

"Silliness," Simon said. Then, almost as an afterthought, "But I would like one of the t-shirts, please."

Eddie stopped the recording before he started laughing, but only just.

"That's awesome," he said. "Thanks. I'm going to tag a staged video of me making potato salad onto the end of that, and it'll go out this afternoon."

"Pleased to oblige. I do want one of the shirts. My nephew's birthday is coming."

"That is a kickass uncle gift. Are you sure you're going to be able to handle the volume of potato salad we're going to need for the event?"

"I won't be doing most of it. Everyone else can peel and slice and such. I'm just there to make sure the herbs all go in, in the proper amounts," Simon reminded him, carrying the pan to the sink and straining the potatoes. "I always liked this recipe. The Queen knew exactly what her people's tastes were."

"Wish I could have met her."

"Me too. I'm curious what you'd make of each other. Probably similar to your and His Highness's first meeting. Maybe less awkward," Simon allowed. "A very gracious woman, Her Majesty. Gone too soon – a very sad illness. Ah, well, but soon we'll have a new king and perhaps a king consort."

"Thanks for the subtle hint, but I figured it out," Eddie said. Simon shot him a sidelong grin. "Hard to believe he's in the market for a husband. He seems pretty married to the job."

"He's asked Alanna to help him find a suitable man," Simon said. Something in his tone caught Eddie's ear.

"Suitable?"

"An arranged marriage. Very traditional but *rather* outmoded." Simon carried the potatoes to a mixing bowl and began shaking them in gently.

"He's looking for a, what, a mail-order prince?" Eddie asked.

"In her words, he wants the whole thing done with," Simon replied. "I'm not worried. She will talk him out of it. Or at least into letting her manage his relationships for him."

"We'd all be in better shape if Alanna managed our lives, probably," Eddie agreed, thoughtful. "Arranged marriage. Not a very good deal for the prince, I feel like."

"How so?" Simon asked.

"Well, we know why he's looking, and *we* know he's a decent guy," Eddie said. "But what kind of person puts themselves up for an arranged marriage with a king they've never met? You get maybe one or two royals who feel like he does, but you're going to have to pick them out of all the con men and attention hounds."

"Royalty is good at sorting the wheat from the chaff. This is fortunate for us," Simon replied.

"Let's hope so. Anyway, not your problem or mine, right?" Eddie asked, though he felt oddly pensive about the idea. Gregory deserved more than a political ally. In private he was kind and fun and intensely vulnerable. It would be too easy for someone to take advantage of that.

On the other hand, most of the really awful ones would probably be scared off by the public nature of it – too much work for some, with the king being a functional part of the political system. What would that job even be like?

"When the queen was alive, what kind of job was it?" he asked. "What did she do, on a daily basis?"

"Ah, Queen Miranda. She did a great many things," Simon told him. "She traveled. Ambassador of culture. She was in several advertisements for national tourism. If the king couldn't attend a social function, she represented him. Eventually she brought the prince to such things to train him."

"She was old blood, though, that's what the prince said. That kind of thing probably has to be picked up when you're a kid."

"They have a saying, actually," Simon said. "The lord's father is the stableman's son."

"Uh…" Eddie frowned, trying to parse this out.

"It means that the best partner for a noble is a commoner," Simon translated. "Destined lovers in Askazer legends are often of different classes. Yes, Gregory's mother was the daughter of an old house, but that house had many maids and butlers marry into it. It's the name that comes down, not the bloodline exactly."

"Like how Prince Gregory is named for a king he isn't related to," Eddie said.

"Exactly. He'll look among the nobility, here and outside the country, but it's also very likely his eventual consort will come from the town, or get off a tourist bus, or have family who sell fish harborside."

"A place after my own heart," Eddie said.

"Mine also. I could never leave here, once I arrived, even if I did have to learn English," Simon said.

"I was going to ask, but it seemed rude. It's a weird country to be speaking English, this deep in mainland Europe," Eddie remarked.

"Bah. Some English colonial nonsense three centuries ago." Simon waved a hand. "I think they kept on after kicking out the English purely to annoy the French."

"Seems to be working," Eddie pointed out.

Simon gaped at him for a second and then laughed. "True! Now," he added, "come with me. You can help me make *real* mayonnaise."

"I have made real mayonnaise before!" Eddie protested, but he followed Simon to the big walk-in fridge for eggs.

THREE WEEKS UNTIL
THE CORONATION OF HIS MAJESTY
KING GREGORY III

IT WASN'T THAT it bothered Eddie, exactly, but the idea of a man like Gregory settling for an arranged marriage – probably to a virtual stranger – gnawed at him. It felt out of character. Not for Crown Prince Gregory or King Gregory III, that was very much in his wheelhouse, but for Gregory the man?

It felt like a building block of the wrong color – it fit the shape, but the design wasn't right. Not that it was Eddie's business, considering they'd already agreed this would be a fun way to pass the time and not a commitment. He'd be gone in less than a full month. Still – Gregory didn't need that and neither did Askazer-Shivadlakia.

The night before Eddie was supposed to present the new picnic idea to Michaelis, Gregory actually came and found him, which he didn't normally; usually Eddie searched him out instead. This time, Gregory turned up in the kitchen after dinner, eating an orange for dessert and watching Simon tidy away the dinner pans while Eddie prepared the picnic basket for the following day. Eddie took the hint and put a little hustle on, then agreed to "a quick meeting in my office" with the prince.

Now, lying in Gregory's bedroom, breathless and relaxed, he let his curiosity get the better of him.

"I feel like I gotta ask you something," he said, "but it's definitely none of my business and probably annoying."

"I'm positive I've heard you ask that kind of question before on your show," Gregory said.

"Have you been watching my show?" Eddie asked, delighted.

"It's streaming," Gregory answered, defensive. "And Alanna said there was one about fried pork belly I had to watch because just seeing it raises your cholesterol."

"Oh yeah. That episode was a lot. But actually most of the questions get cleared beforehand. I'm not a journalist, I'm just a hungry dude. And I don't know them. Not as well as I know you, anyway," he said. He watched Gregory consider this.

"You might as well ask. If I don't want to answer it, I simply won't."

"Is it true you're going to get Alanna to find you a husband?"

Gregory let out a bark of laughter, a shock reaction. "Did she tell you that?"

"Simon said you're considering an arranged marriage."

"That's more accurate. Sure, I have a meeting about it set for after the coronation."

"Why?" Eddie asked. "I mean, if you were just a dude that might be different, but you're the king. Royalty mates for life, usually. It's a big mess if they don't."

"So?"

"So you want to spend your life hitched to a stranger?"

"Don't we all, in some way or another?" Gregory asked. "We're very, very lucky if we get to choose our bosses. Friends start out as strangers. There are politicians in my cabinet I would prefer I didn't have to work with, but until they die or I do, here we are."

"But this is a life mate. Someone you're going to sleep next to."

"It's much more important that I'm going to work next to them," Gregory said, eyes dark but not sad, exactly. Perhaps a little resigned. "I'd love to marry for love but time is fleeting and it's a little impractical."

"Well, I'm not here to throw stones. I'm just curious," Eddie said. Gregory gave him a smile.

"Some would say I'm young to commit my whole life to governing the country," he said. "It's a much more complicated, difficult thing than a marriage. And – and if someone did love me, my duty is to the country. It'd be hard on him."

"Your parents did okay."

"Let you in on a secret," Gregory said, inching closer. Eddie leaned in. "They were absolutely in a threesome with the country."

It was Eddie's turn to laugh in shock. "Gregory!"

"It's true. A love like that, where we both loved each other *and* the work, I'd jump for in a minute, but the odds aren't on my side. So, I'll find someone agreeable, who likes the country and puts up with me, and we'll figure the rest out as we go."

"Well, it's your life," Eddie said. "I have a suggestion, though."

"I'm all ears."

"You are…" Eddie narrowed his eyes, pausing for effect, "…*amazingly* good at sex. I'm going to suggest that you make sure whoever you end up with, they appreciate this about you. You can't waste your talents on an unappreciative audience."

"Well, that's very flattering. I'll do my best," Gregory said, rolling over to kiss him. "In the meantime I'm happy to share."

The following evening, King Michaelis and Crown Prince Gregory took a stroll through the palace, starting in the rarely-used throne room and following the path that, presumably, attending visitors would take to the garden.

"What've you got planned?" Michaelis asked, but Gregory just grinned at him.

Outside, on the flat stretch of grass and flowerbeds of the west garden, bordered by hedges, a single elegant table was standing, covered with a tablecloth in the checked blue-and-orange of the flag. Behind it, slightly to one side, stood two waiters, each holding a thermos, and Eddie, holding a printed-out menu. On the table was a picnic basket. As they arrived, Eddie pulled out one of the chairs.

"Your Majesty, Your Highness," he said. "I have a new concept for the coronation banquet to show you."

Michaelis gave him and then the chair a measured look, but he stepped up to the table and allowed himself to be seated. Gregory sat himself, eyes on his father, hoping a more immersive experience would help.

"Prince Gregory said something to me that inspired me," Eddie continued. "He liked the idea, so we thought we'd give you the practical demonstration."

"On the lawn?" Michaelis asked. Eddie nodded. "Well, I'm interested."

The king reached for the picnic basket, tipping it towards himself to unpack it. The wine came out first; with long habit Michaelis handed it to Gregory, who took a corkscrew from Eddie to open it while his father unpacked the rest. There were small packages wrapped in white paper, little jars of mustard and slightly larger ones of pickles, a pot of soft cheese, a bowl of fresh fruit.

"Allow me to present to you an elegant, full service, traditional coronation picnic," Eddie said, as the waiters came forward. They laid a pair of bowls in front of each man, one pouring soup while the other gently spooned potato salad. Michaelis unwrapped one of the paper packages, studying the finger sandwich with interest until he saw the potato salad.

"I told Eddie about how we used to have it when we went fishing," Gregory said quietly.

Michaelis nodded, picking up a fork, taking a small bite. Gregory stifled amusement at the idea of his father knowing the one-bite rule.

"I want you to picture this whole field full of tables – six to eight seats per. Each table has a basket with sandwiches, fruit, assorted other foods and wine," Eddie said. "Music, dancing…everyone's happy to be celebrating the coronation. Your favorite soup – "

"And the queen's favorite picnic food," Michaelis finished. For a half a second, Gregory wondered if the whole idea touched a nerve, if the reminder of his mother was a little too painful. But then Michaelis tilted his head to look up at the chef, and his face was thoughtful, not pained. Slowly, his eyes crinkled, a smile crossing his face. "Well, she would have loved this idea."

"I'm glad to hear it," Eddie said sincerely.

"Croquet," Michaelis added, and Eddie's smile turned puzzled.

"Come again?"

"Ask Alanna where the croquet sets are," Michaelis said. "We have a number of them. And I believe some kites, as well. For the children. We can purchase some if there aren't any."

"I will…absolutely do that," Eddie said. He glanced at Gregory, who tried to telegraph calm. If his father was making contributions, then he'd made up his mind to approve.

"It's been ages since we had a garden party," Michaelis said.

"A picnic, dad," Gregory replied.

"It's a garden party," Michaelis declared, and Gregory made a choice not to die on that hill. "Have Alanna find some appropriate live music. Hire extra waitstaff if needed. Very well done, Mr. Rambler."

"Thank you, Your Majesty," Eddie said.

"You can go up to the kitchen," Michaelis said to Eddie, and then to the waiters hovering nearby, "You as well. We'll bring in the plates when we're done."

Eddie, clearly reassured, retreated with the staff. Gregory took a bite of the potato salad, as good as it ever was.

"I really liked this idea," he said, as his father tried the soup.

"Yes, so do I. It's very suitable," Michaelis said. "And also pleasant," he added tolerantly, when Gregory opened his mouth. "I know that's important to you. Clearly so does this chef."

"He's a thoughtful man, once you get to know him," Gregory said.

"Well, I did always try to teach you to dig deep. It's a wise king who looks for the truth, let alone finds it."

"That's a really high bar to set right now," Gregory said. "I was hoping for the first few years we'd just be happy if I don't get voted out. A quest for an objective truth is more of a fifteen-years-into-a-golden-age kind of a thing."

"I waited at least ten before I did mine," Michaelis agreed.

"And what objective truth did you find, Dad?" Gregory asked. Michaelis looked up and around, thoughtful.

"I couldn't say," he said. "But you were born about ten years into the reign, if that helps."

Eddie was waiting for them when they came inside. He wasn't obvious about it; the kitchen was empty as they put their plates in the sink and the basket on the counter, but Gregory saw him lurking near the back entrance and told his father to go on ahead, that he'd see him for breakfast tomorrow. As soon as Michaelis was gone, Eddie emerged, fists clenched in triumph.

"He loved it, right? He totally did. You have to actually give me the high five this time," he said, and held up his hand. Gregory gave him as good an imitation of his father as he could muster, looking him up and down, then raised one hand to tap his palm lightly against Eddie's.

"I knew it," Eddie crowed, breaking into an ugly, enthusiastic dance move. "Man this is going to be a slam dunk, easiest dinner I ever catered. We're gonna be under budget, I'm gonna look like a boss, and you are going to have a really great banquet," he said, dancing around Gregory. "They're gonna think you are the coolest. Am I in charge of buying the kites or is that an Alanna job?"

"She'll assign it to staff," Gregory said. "I'm pretty sure they'll have to buy new croquet sets anyway. We used to use them to tap the fig trees to get the ripe ones down before harvest. We definitely destroyed at least two sets."

"Aw, tiny Gregory with a big wooden mallet, beating on a fig tree. I wish there was footage," Eddie said.

"Thankfully, there isn't. That was very well done, Eddie," Gregory said. "He's fully in. There was some feedback on the sandwiches and he'll undoubtedly have notes about the wine pairings but I will pay you extra to be tolerant."

"No need. I'm happy to hear his thoughts. The royal sommelier had some strong opinions on the wine too," Eddie said, calming himself down. "Okay. So. Tomorrow, I'm going to have to shift into high-gear asskicking mode. Do you want to celebrate tonight, or should I come find you in a couple of days after I've gone on a blitz of food-buying and menu preparation?"

"Come by tonight," Gregory said, tilting his head in the direction of his rooms. "Give me an hour or so? I have to wrap up a few things."

"Sure. I'll spend the time coming up with a secret knock," Eddie said.

"I'm on pins and needles," Gregory told him. He leaned in briefly, stealing a kiss, and then left the kitchen with a spring in his step, while Eddie redoubled his triumphant dancing.

The knock, when it came, was quiet, but also extravagant and complicated, really more of a drum solo; it was still going on when Gregory opened the door.

Eddie, both fists upraised and knuckles at the ready, beamed at him and let his arms fall, then bent to pick up a carton next to his feet.

"This is, technically, business," he said, brushing past Gregory into the room. "You are being crowned king, which is a big deal, Sweet Prince, and that calls for champagne."

"Isn't 'sweet prince' from *Hamlet*?" Gregory asked.

"It is," Eddie agreed, pulling tiny piccolo-bottles of champagne out of the carton.

"And isn't it what his friend calls him when he's dying?"

"Goodnight, sweet prince, and flights of angels sing thee to thy rest," Eddie agreed. "It's also what you're supposed to quote to lift the curse if you've said 'Macbeth' inside a theater. It's a turn of phrase, gorgeous. The point is, I have some champagne for you to sample, both so that we can celebrate and so that you can choose what you'd like served for your toasts."

Out came a series of tasting glasses, as well as a bowl of coffee beans and a sleeve of saltine crackers.

"Sip lightly, swallow, give me your notes, then sniff the coffee, eat a piece of cracker, and rinse your mouth with water," Eddie said, as he began opening bottles. "You can spit if you want, but I didn't bring a bucket."

"You've done this before," Gregory said.

"Yes, but not often. Believe it or not, there's not a lot of call for wine tasting in burger joints," Eddie said, offering him the first glass.

The tasting was fun; with a little of the pressure off he could enjoy the flavors and the zing of the bubbles. All but one of the wines were true champagne, and the last one was a California sparkling wine that Eddie explained came from a vineyard where he had an investment.

"Just for fun," he said, and Gregory leaned into him, warm and tipsy from the drink.

"You are fun," he agreed. Eddie laughed.

"I do my best," he said. "Enjoy this. I won't be around as much for a while."

"I am." Gregory inched closer, until Eddie put an arm around his shoulders. "I'll miss you when you leave."

"You won't have time. I've seen your schedule. And anyway, I'll be back," Eddie said. "Now that I know what a hot spot this place is, I'll have to film an episode here. Maybe do a whole season in Europe.

What passes for diner food in these parts?"

"Couldn't say. I'm sure you'll sniff it out, though."

Eddie laughed into his hair. "I am good at that. You'll let me do at least one segment in the palace though, right? My loyal fans will know if you don't. They recognize the kitchen now."

"As long as you promise not to poach Simon," Gregory said.

"Simon wouldn't leave even if you fired him."

"Nice to have loyal staff."

"Loyal hell, he just knows he's never gonna get his hands on appliances that nice anywhere else."

Gregory laughed hard enough to snort, and then laughed at that. Eddie was warm under him, and for at least a little while the kingdom could look after itself.

"C'mon, let's get you to bed," Eddie said, half-lifting him and dragging them both to the bedroom. "You can miss me all you want tomorrow."

TWO WEEKS UNTIL
THE CORONATION OF HIS MAJESTY
KING GREGORY III

AFTER THE MENU was approved, the time flew by. Gregory saw Eddie less than he'd like; he was distracted with interviews and photo sessions, logistics meetings for the coronation, and multiplying meetings as his father handed off duties one by one. Still, he tried to sidetrack whatever walk-and-talk he was on so that they passed the kitchen. If Eddie saw him wave, he'd grin and wave back. If he didn't, it was generally because he was so deep into something that he didn't notice, so at least he was keeping busy as well.

"I don't think there were nearly this many pressmen at my coronation," Michaelis said one afternoon, coming into the office as a cameraman and his partner left. "I'm not sure if I should be jealous."

"I wouldn't. There's just more...I don't know, news, now," Gregory said, waving a hand. "And when Eddie put us on Photogram, it got a lot of people interested. I think there's ten or twenty real, proper influencers who are going to feature us. The cafes in town are keeping track of how many foreigners call them cute and authentic."

"Influencers," Michaelis said, rolling his eyes. "They didn't have that when I was crowned, either."

"I've been thinking of becoming one. It doesn't seem overly difficult, especially if you've got a palace," Gregory said with a grin. Michaelis nodded, amused. "You could host a podcast. Talk about statecraft, diplomacy. Pressuring your son into running the country."

"I pressured you!" Michaelis pretended outrage. "When you were *five* you told me you wanted to be king."

"And what a mistake that proved to be," Gregory drawled. "Did you need something?"

"Not in particular, just to see how you were holding up."

Gregory tapped the end of his pen on his blotter. "Doing all right, actually. There's less waiting around now, and things seem to be going smoothly. Busy, but tolerable."

"I'm glad to hear it. The rest of the palace is going wild. Can't walk through a door but someone runs past with bunting or place settings or some damn thing."

"Ah yes. Alanna's been scarce, I thought that might be why."

"That chef has everyone on the jump." Michaelis studied him. "He's very enthusiastic about the garden party."

"He's just pleased you liked it. So am I."

His father seemed about to say something else, then changed his mind. "Well, it's one small moment in what I think will be a very long reign. They trot out that old footage of me being crowned once a year, but nobody remembers all the details anymore, and thank goodness. Try not to blaspheme or fall on your face and you'll be fine."

"What even counts as blasphemy anymore?" Gregory wondered aloud, as Michaelis rose to leave.

"You'd know better than I would," Michaelis told him. "Come to breakfast tomorrow, I want to see you eat a full meal."

"Promise, Dad," Gregory said, and Michaelis lifted his hand in acknowledgment as he left. Gregory heard Alanna call a greeting to the king, and then she was ducking into the office, tablet at the ready.

"Well, it appears I have open office hours," Gregory said as she sat down. "Keeping busy, I hear."

"Yes, but no disasters yet. Probably means there's going to be one right beforehand, but it'll be useful on my resume eventually," she said.

"You're not pulled too tight?" Gregory asked. Her smile softened.

"No, I'm fine. It's reminding me how much I love planning parties and how very happy I am I don't do it for a living," she said.

"Dad said Eddie has the staff 'on the jump'," Gregory said.

"I think they're all breathing a sigh of relief he'll be gone for a couple of days," she said, and Gregory frowned.

"Gone?"

"He might not have told you – there's an issue with the, ah, mushroom supply," she said, checking her notes. "He's going to drive down the coast, try and buy up any he can find in bulk. It'll take a few days to get to Messina and back."

"No, I hadn't heard. I hope it's a productive trip."

"I think he wanted to get out of the palace, give everyone a breather, maybe take some time for himself, too," she confided. "It must be hard, coming all the way out here for two months."

"Well, he travels a lot, I suppose he's used to it," Gregory said, wondering why Eddie hadn't told him. True, they hadn't seen each other much, but he would have wanted to know – he could have arranged for a car, and staff to help if he wanted it –

Which was of course when Eddie knocked on the open door.

"Your Highness," he said, and then with a nod, "Hey Al!"

"Eddie," she replied. "I was just telling Gregory about your trip down the coast."

"Oh yeah! Man, I wish you could come, but it's a little more than a jaunt to Fons-Askaz," Eddie said. "Don't worry, though, I'll be back in plenty of time. I was coming to let you know about it. Should have known Alanna would get here first."

"Will you be all right driving?" Gregory asked.

"Oh, sure. Simon's lending me his car. I've heard tall tales about Italian driving but I grew up in California, I should be fine."

"Sounds like quite the trip," Gregory said with a grin that was only half-forced. "Come find me when you return, I'd like to see these mushrooms you're on a mission to find."

"Will do, boss," Eddie said, and trotted off, probably back to the kitchen. It took Gregory a second to register the look on Alanna's face.

"No," he said, pointing at her.

"Oh yes," Alanna said.

"Alanna, do not – "

"The dive bar chef is the *amore!*" she cried.

"The what?" he asked, startled.

"Jerry and I called your mystery boyfriend the *amore* and it's the guy who *you said* was more dive bar than gastropub!"

"He's not my boyfriend and I'm not having this conversation with you," he told her. "Besides, I didn't know him then."

"You're dating the chef! It's just like Gregory II's father did, you remember we had to learn about it in history…"

"It's nothing like that," Gregory said, trying for dignity and probably failing. "It's not a romance. I've told you that much! It's just…convenient."

"I hope it's more than convenient," Alanna said. "I mean I hope it's fun. He seems like he'd be fun."

Gregory sighed. "Yes. He is fun. And being honest, last week I think it kept me sane."

"I know! I just didn't know it was him," Alanna said.

"You can't tell anyone, Al. It's nobody's business."

It was her turn for dignity. "You insult us both by suggesting I'd tattle. I wouldn't do that to you or him."

"I don't even want you talking to Eddie about it, I don't want to make it any weirder than it already is."

Alanna got up and rested against the desk, leaning over him "One, you could not make it weirder if you tried, because you're super weird. Two, Eddie's a nice guy, so I hope you've talked with him about the temporary nature of this."

"I have, I promise."

"Good. Three," she added, standing and heading for the door, "I want you to think about this moment in a couple of months when you propose, in all seriousness, an arranged marriage."

Gregory sighed. "Message received, Al."

"Just so it is."

When she was gone, Gregory leaned back in his chair and stared at the ceiling. He didn't want it to be weird; in fact, he wanted it to be as normal as it could be. If he weren't king, or if Eddie weren't famous and living on another continent most of the time…well, one couldn't invite someone to immigrate on five weeks of acquaintance, and Gregory *was* king, or nearly. He and Eddie were on different paths. That happened, and you simply had to enjoy the paths before they diverged. With any luck, he'd meet a couple of prospective king consorts he'd like just as well as Eddie, but who could actually stay in Askazer-Shivadlakia.

"Holy crow, friends and fans," Eddie said, sitting in a taverna that had agreeably allowed him to film there in return for some publicity. "Did you all ever think I'd be coming to you from Messina, Italy?"

He pointed up and around him in all directions. "I didn't even know Messina was a real place until like…probably college," he said. "And that's not my fault! Half of Shakespeare's plays are set in real places and the other half are in like, whatever, fairyland, and you never know which is which. In case you're wondering, *Much Ado About Nothing* is set in Messina, which is real, and it is also where this video is set."

He grinned at the camera. "I'm here on a mission to get some mushrooms, but if I had a little more time or budget this would absolutely be an episode of *Truly Tasty*. So I'm going to give you a little mini-episode and cut here to a cooking tutorial in the kitchen right….now," he said, and hit stop on the video. The cooking tutorial, by the taverna's hip young owner, was already in the can, and he joined up the two videos and tossed them on Photogram.

One of the best things about Photogram was that if you posted, people knew where you were. His parents never worried about him if he had posted there within the last twelve hours, and it was easy to let people know you'd reached your destination safely. He wondered if Gregory had a notification set up, or just saw them whenever he happened to think of it.

Nuts; he was here to buy mushrooms and see the city, not worry about the king-to-be. It was one reason among many other and probably saner reasons that he'd decided on the trip. He was into the crown prince, in a way he recognized was more than just surface attraction, but Eddie himself had been the one to suggest it could just be a good time. Couldn't go back on that now. It wasn't fair to Greg, and it wouldn't exactly be easy on Eddie either.

No, he'd take a few days to get out of the palace, and when he came back he'd be in a shallower state of mind. He could hang out with the crown prince, who among other things badly needed a little pressure release, and who in any case was a lot of fun to be around. They'd finish up the affair, say fond and already-nostalgic goodbyes, and in a hundred years Eddie could tell his grandkids he'd shacked up with a prince, and nobody would believe him.

His phone rang, a number that wasn't in his contacts, and he picked up with a cheerful, "Yello!"

"Eddie," Gregory's voice was both amused and dry.

"Uh oh, what'd I do now," Eddie said.

"I saw the video. You're supposed to be here for Askazer-

Shivadlakia, not canoodling around with Messina."

"She means nothing to me," Eddie said dramatically. "It was the heat of the moment."

"Hm, it was the smell of the pasta, I have a feeling," Gregory answered.

"The things they do with fettucini," Eddie replied, lowering his voice and leaning into the phone. "I should have come to Italy when I was like twelve."

"Pretty sure you were still in school at twelve."

"Not if I could help it. Anyway, it's just the one video. I'll be back tomorrow. Day after tomorrow in the morning, at the latest."

"Did you find your mushrooms?"

"And then some. Almost positive none of them will kill you."

"It would be highly operatic to be poisoned at my own coronation, but yes, I'd like to avoid that fate," Gregory said.

Eddie grinned. "Only the best for the king. Hey, can I call you later tonight?"

"What, you aren't going drinking with that chef from your video?"

It struck Eddie that the prince was jealous, which was hilarious. "Yeah, but you know you'll be my first call when I'm maudlin drunk."

There was a pause, and then Gregory cleared his throat. "Look, this is a favor you absolutely don't have to do."

"What is it?"

"Don't go out tonight. Get yourself a cup of gelato and have an early night instead," Gregory said. "Or don't, it's a stupid request – "

"I'm not especially stoked to get drunk with chefs. Having been a chef, I know what we're like," Eddie said. "Gelato and an early night, no problem."

"That's all right?"

"It's fine, Greg," Eddie said. "Good excuse, actually. See you tomorrow, huh?"

"Tomorrow," Gregory echoed, and hung up. Eddie put his phone on the table and sat back, considering.

Well. Gregory ben Michaelis, crown prince of Askazer-Shivadlakia, missed him and didn't want him going out with someone else. Flattering, and touching too; Eddie liked Gregory and enjoyed the idea that Gregory liked him as much. Trouble, of course, it was trouble in a couple of ways, but it was also nice to be missed.

The truth was that being a celebrity was fun, but it wasn't why he'd gone into show business. He liked teaching people about the world, and experiencing it as he did so. He was already tired of being on the road so much; he'd done enough *Truly Tasty* to get a sense of American cuisine, and what newcomers were bringing to it. If he wanted to settle down, maybe start a real cooking show in a kitchen of his own, he could. He'd always figured it'd be in America – Hollywood or New York, or even somewhere like Austin or Chicago. But…here he was, in Italy. Askazer-Shivadlakia was within spitting distance of Italy and France, two great countries for food. It had a climate like his home in California, and a leader that really seemed to care about agriculture and food and the links between them.

I could stay there, he thought. *It'd be dumb, but I've been dumber.*

On the other hand, no need to overstay his welcome. It was probably less cool a place if you were a resident who had to pay taxes and take out your own trash and stuff. He'd maybe get back to the palace faster than he'd intended, but then he'd cook this meal, celebrate the coronation, and head back to America to consider his next move.

Alanna came in as Gregory was hanging up with Eddie, and she grinned annoyingly at him.

"We are too old and our friendship is too valuable to me to fire you out of spite, but I haven't ruled out having you framed for sedition," he said.

"Greg, I love you, but you couldn't frame a poster without my help," she replied.

"I'm about to be king of a whole entire country."

"Try doing that without your to-do list," she said, and he gestured defeat. "Was that Eddie?"

"As though you didn't know," he replied.

"He has a very audible phone voice," she admitted. "Sounded like he missed you."

"Did it?" he asked, a little wistful.

"Sounds like you miss him, for sure," she said.

"He'll be back tomorrow, so he says."

"Faster than expected. So why are you sulking in your sulk fortress?" she asked.

"I'm not sulking. I'm just…considering everything," he replied. "The coronation's getting closer, lots of stuff is happening. Things are moving very fast."

"This sounds silly to say," she said, "but you're only king of one very small country."

"And not even that yet. No, I know. It's a big job, but not President of the United States big."

"At least you're a useful king," she said. "Are you getting cold feet about it? Or is this something else?"

He folded his arms on the desk, resting his chin on them, slumped over. "Remember when you told me to think about how I'm sort-of dating Eddie when I think about that arranged-marriage meeting?"

She nodded, the amused expression fading from her face.

"It's months away. I don't know why I'm thinking of it. But…"

"Difficult to consider the idea when you've got someone you like close to hand?" she asked.

"I do like him. But it isn't that way and it can't be."

"You keep saying that," Alanna replied, raising an eyebrow. "But you don't ever really say why. I get not wanting to just blurt out that he isn't marriage material again – "

"He isn't marriage material *for me*. I like him. I think he's nice and funny. He's less intense in person than he is on his show."

"I have to say I watched the show and I still didn't expect him to be so…real," she agreed.

"That's the problem, though!" Gregory said, sitting back again, looking up at the ceiling. "He's *so* real. He's a person, not a political prop, and even if I wanted him to be that, he never could. He never *would*. He has no other way of being, he's not a diplomat or a royal. He has no manners, he has no training for something like this. He grew up on a beach in California. He's a TV star. He's a *tacky* TV star. It's something he's proud of."

"Why shouldn't he be?"

"Well, exactly," Gregory said. "But I have to be honest about how that would probably go. I can't consider people who wouldn't be suited to the throne."

Alanna was quiet for long enough that he looked at her curiously. She was thoughtful, clearly considering something.

"With all due respect," she said finally, "And I'm saying this both as your friend and as your employee, I think you're wrong about Eddie. In a couple of ways."

"How so?"

"I think he'd make a great royal. People love him. He makes that easy. He might work hard at making it easy, but he does it, and he seems to enjoy it. People genuinely like him, because he's genuinely likeable. Not just Americans, either. Your subjects love him."

"You can't be serious," he said. "You've told me what he's dragged us into. All the influencers and such."

"They know that's not his fault, and they like that he loves the country enough to want to share it. Honestly...you and your father have to make the laws, you have to make unpopular decisions sometimes, and they get that, but they don't have to like you," Alanna pointed out. "They already voted for you. Eddie's like the fun parent. He's spent a lot of time here, talking to people. Learning about the food. He hasn't imported a single thing for the banquet except these mushrooms and even then it's only because we didn't have enough. The food's all local, and so is the decoration. The picnic baskets are from a basket weaver in town. I didn't even know we had a basket weaver."

"How'd he find them, then?" Gregory asked, distracted.

"I have no idea. No clue where he got all his new ideas about dairy farming, either, but the milk board is interested. And he knows more than you think," she added, before Gregory could follow that tangent down a rabbit hole. "Ever notice he always addresses you and your father properly? He always gets your titles right."

Gregory thought back. He hadn't noticed, probably because he was used to it. But it was telling that Alanna had.

"Remember when he had the kids in to do the cookies?" she asked. He nodded. "After they made the cookies, he took them on a palace tour. He had a lot of stuff written on his hand, but he was very enthusiastic about it."

"Did you go on this tour?" Gregory asked.

"Well, I'd eaten the cookies, I couldn't skip the tour," Alanna said reasonably. "The point is, whether or not you want to marry a guy you've only known five weeks, he has the skills a royal spouse needs. I'm not saying you should and definitely I doubt he would, but I don't think you should write off the idea wholesale."

"I don't know if people would find him as whimsical on a throne as they do in a kitchen," Gregory said.

"Do you think they'd do better with some stranger you don't even know that well?" she asked.

"If the stranger is the better partner, they should. I have to put the country first," Gregory pointed out.

"Then you definitely shouldn't be dating a guy who brought a bunch of tourists here," Alanna replied, voice tart.

"Alanna."

"Your grandfather was a commoner when he became king. I know his wife's parents weren't thrilled with him being their son-in-law *or* the king, but he won the vote and he's a famous, beloved legend now. Putting the country first means listening to what it actually needs, not what you think it should need."

Gregory studied the ceiling. "Well, it's a nice idea."

"You know I've got your back whatever you decide. Eddie Rambler isn't your last chance for a relationship unless you make him your last chance, and I don't think he'd love it if you did. But if you're doing a husband-search you could do a lot worse."

"I do listen to you, you know," he said. "I'll think about it."

"That's all I can ask," she said. "I'll see you for breakfast, huh?"

"I'll be there."

"Goodnight, Your Highness."

When she was gone, he stretched, rose, and closed the window, locking the office up after himself.

It *was* a nice idea. But not exactly practical.

Eddie arrived at the palace after dinner the next day. Gregory caught a glimpse of him through a window, unloading box after box of mushrooms from the car, in dirt-smeared shirtsleeves and a wrinkled pair of cargo shorts. He looked so good that Gregory caught his breath, and then felt stupid for thinking a t-shirt and cargo shorts were sexy. But the flex of Eddie's arms carrying the boxes in was nice to look at. And the easy way he moved, at home here already, made all of Gregory's resolutions to continue to treat this lightly very difficult to keep.

"Hey!" Eddie said, as Gregory stepped out of the side door to greet him. "Good timing! Here," he said, and plopped a box into Gregory's hands. He took it out of instinct, then stared down at it.

"How many mushrooms are you feeding us?" he asked.

"They cook down a lot," Eddie said. "Plus, I figured if I'm cleaning you out of mushrooms so completely I've gotta go to Italy for more, I might as well get everything I can. Anything we don't need, I'll dry them and you can give them out to your subjects as a coronation gift. But I really gave them to you just now so I could do this," he added, and leaned over the box, kissing Gregory briefly. It was fast and discreet enough that Gregory almost wished he'd taken a little longer. "You'd have loved the drive and hated me stopping to take selfies every ten minutes on the way down."

"Probably," Gregory agreed, as Eddie took another box from the back of the car, leading the way inside. "I'm glad you enjoyed yourself."

"I'm definitely going to need to do a show in Italy," Eddie said as he set the mushrooms down in a corner with the other boxes. "Maybe a special miniseries of some kind. I could call it Rambling Down Italy."

"Keep It Noodle," Gregory said, and Eddie burst out laughing as he went outside to lock up the car.

"That's good! I'm stealing that," he said. "Glad to be back, though. Italy's been around for a couple thousand years, it can wait, and I have cooking to do here and…"

He leaned in close, holding up a paper-wrapped object from his pocket.

"Let me make you breakfast in bed tomorrow," he said quietly. "I have a truffle."

"Just what every young man loves to hear," Gregory replied, but he kept his voice soft too. "I'd like that."

"Then let me shower and get changed, and I'll drop in," Eddie suggested. Gregory nodded. "Okay. I'm gonna go make sure the mushrooms are stored and let Simon know I'll pay for the interior detailing on his car. Wait for the secret knock."

"It's really more of a drum solo," Gregory said, but Eddie just laughed and ducked back into the kitchen.

Eddie did the drum solo about forty minutes later, but he also let himself in when it was done; Gregory, who'd brought a few reports up to his rooms to read while he waited, set them aside and made space for him on the couch while Eddie put a small bag of food in the refrigerator of the kitchenette.

"Do you ever get to stop working?" Eddie asked, coming to join him on the couch. He sounded less petulant than many would have — more curious, like he was…concerned, almost.

"Eventually," Gregory said. "I mean, most nights."

"But it won't be like this for you when you're king, all these fifteen hour days? I realize this is hypocritical coming from a chef, but at least when I'm filming I get mandated union breaks."

"Oh — yes, this is temporary. There's just a lot to take in, a lot of transition plans to make," he said. "Some staff are leaving when my father does, so this week I've also been looking at resumes and considering revisions to our pension plan. And there's a lot of decisions to make for the coronation even now."

"Mm, which crown to wear?"

"Fortunately that one's out of my hands, but you're not far off. Decor for the throne room, finishing touches on speeches, making the final call on seating arrangements."

"Seems a little beneath you," Eddie observed.

"Well, sometimes two of the people attending have parents who hate each other, and you just have to seat them together and hope for the best because a third person needs a seat at a different table so that nobody gets stabbed over certain votes taken ten years ago they're still mad about. Sometimes you have to shuffle the feuding members of a family so that they can't needle each other about who got Granny's good china. Babysitting petulant petty nobility won't be the majority of my job, but it's probably good practice regardless."

"Maybe a lottery would be easier. Pull a number and let the chips fall. If people fight, they fight. A stabbing would probably liven things up," Eddie said. "Although it's hard to enjoy my cooking when that kind of shenanigan is happening."

"Don't tell me it's the first time you've been in the kitchen when someone's been stabbed," Gregory replied. Eddie laughed and grabbed him, pulling him over to straddle his lap.

"I've lived a sordid life, for sure," he said, hands firmly on Gregory's hips. "But I feel like I'm moving up in the world lately."

"Ah," Gregory bent to kiss him. "Kept man of the crown prince. I see."

"Am I?" Eddie asked, amused. "You did seem very jealous of my Italian friend in Messina."

"Well, I don't get you for very long," Gregory said, and something in Eddie's face made him uncomfortable enough to add, hurriedly, "And I was concerned about the mushroom expenditure."

"I kept all the receipts," Eddie said, whatever feeling he'd been having flitting away. "Anyway, let me prove to you I missed you."

"I'd very much like that," Gregory told him, and bent in for another kiss.

The next morning, Gregory woke to a clank and a swear-word, and rolled over in bed to find Eddie rummaging in the kitchenette. He'd located a frying pan and a mixing bowl, but seemed to be on a quest for something more complicated.

"I don't have a stand mixer," he called, and Eddie straightened from his inspection of a cupboard.

"I'd be horrified by that but Simon has three, so the ratio of stand mixers to residents in the palace is okay," he said. "Do you have a mandoline slicer?"

Gregory grunted, sitting up. "I have no idea."

"Well, I'll make do," Eddie decided, cracking eggs into the bowl. Gregory noticed the precious paper-wrapped truffle sitting nearby.

"You didn't actually have to make me breakfast," he said.

"And give Simon first crack at the truffle?" Eddie threw him a smile over his shoulder. "French toast or scrambled eggs? I brought fixings for both."

"French toast, please," Gregory said, and Eddie nodded. While Eddie cooked, he checked his phone – no urgent emails, no impending disasters – and put on a robe, settling back on the bed when Eddie brought him a plate. The french toast was lacey at the edges, a delicate brown with gold highlights, and atop each piece were paper-thin shreds of truffle.

"You do, fortunately, have sharp knives," Eddie said, settling across from him with his own plate. Gregory took a mouthful, enjoying the earthy bite of the truffle against the gold crunch of the fried bread.

"They don't get much use," he said. "I'm not what you'd call an enthusiastic cook."

"Well, nobody's perfect," Eddie said. Gregory rolled his eyes. "If you were an enthusiastic cook I'd honestly start to be worried. Royalty, politician, bowfisher, and he looks good in a suit. If you could cook, too, you'd be some kind of experimental clone. Do you sing?"

"And play the piano, neither especially well," Gregory said. "Little hypocritical of you to ask, don't you think?"

"What's that mean?" Eddie asked, pretending to be wounded.

"Shakespeare-quoting, truffle-hunting celebrity, a TV star and influencer and he *can* cook?" Gregory recited, in a decent approximation of Eddie's accent. "What else do you do, appraise gemstones and raise racing pigeons?"

"If it helps, several people have tried and failed to teach me to knit," Eddie said.

"Off with his head," Gregory replied soberly. Eddie laughed as he took another bite of his breakfast. "I was thinking, though."

"I'm in trouble now."

"Eddie, really," Gregory protested. Eddie subsided. "I know this coming week leading up to the coronation is going to be busy for both of us. But if something goes wrong, or if you need me to back you on something, come find me."

Eddie nodded, considering this as he swallowed. "Deal, but I have a condition."

"Oh?"

"I want to know you're eating and resting, and I can't do that myself. If necessary I will sic Jerry on you."

Gregory gave him a half-smile.

"So if I don't see you in the family dining room for at least one meal a day, I'm gonna break out the big guns, okay?" Eddie tilted his head. "And that's not part of the job. It's because I like you and I see how hard you work. Can't have the king passing out during the coronation, either, it'd really harsh the reception."

"I'll do my best," Gregory said. "Though I will also say it is possible to bribe me with desserts."

"I'll bear that in mind," Eddie replied, laughing.

ONE WEEK UNTIL
THE CORONATION OF HIS MAJESTY
KING GREGORY III

GREGORY WAS ASLEEP, or rather barely on the verge of awareness. He knew he was warm. The sheets were soft, and he could feel the light weight of the blanket on top of him, insulating him from the world.

And then Eddie Rambler called, "GOOD MORNING!"

Gregory opened his eyes just in time for Eddie to peel back the blankets, uncovering his head and shoulders. The light in the room was dim, but still enough to make him squint.

"Up and at 'em," Eddie said. "It's a busy day for me and probably the last time I'll get to see you for very long until the coronation."

"Why?" Gregory asked, more of a plea to the universe than a request for explanation.

"It's crunch time. This morning I need to drive into town and I think you should come along. Keep me company."

"Town?" Gregory managed.

"We gotta load up on picnic baskets and haul them back here so the kitchen staff can start packing them," Eddie explained, correctly interpreting his question. "Simon's busy boiling every potato ever, and the rest of the staff are helping when they can, but they've still got regular meals to serve."

"Mm." Gregory swung himself mostly out of bed, groping for his robe. Eddie put a mug of coffee in his hand instead. "Thank you. This wouldn't have anything to do with me missing dinner yesterday, would it?"

"I told you if you didn't have at least one meal a day in the family dining room, I'd be forced to take action," Eddie said.

"I meant to. I did eat."

"I know, or I would have done this last night."

"Not that I'm not glad to see you, but you are a lot first thing in the morning."

"Baby, I'm a lot all day," Eddie said, and Gregory couldn't disagree.

He hadn't seen Eddie much since his triumphant return from mushroom-hunting, but then neither of them had much time to spare at this point. As he dressed one-handed, sipping from the coffee cup in his other hand, Eddie gave him a rundown on what he'd done and what he still had to do – which Gregory suspected was more for Eddie than for himself. What had been prepped, what was left to prep, and what was currently in progress meant much more to Eddie, logistically, than it did to him.

Caffeinated and dressed, he trooped after Eddie towards the garage, but put out a hand to stop him from taking Simon's car again. Instead, Gregory pulled the dust-sheet off a pickup truck at the back.

"We can take my car," he said.

"Your car?" Eddie asked, studying the battered vehicle.

"It has more cargo space," Gregory explained.

"Does it have a floor?"

"Don't be so picky." Gregory hoisted himself into the driver's seat, taking the key off the dashboard, and Eddie clambered up into the other side. The truck engine purred when he turned the ignition, to Eddie's surprise (and a little to Gregory's). He eased it out of the garage and onto the main road leading away from the palace.

"I learned to drive in this car," he said, as they bounced down the road.

"I'm gaining a new respect for you and your secret, reckless disregard for your own life," Eddie replied.

"I think the gardener had it before I did. But it's pretty good for running around the countryside when I don't want the pomp and circumstance of an official motorcade."

"Yeah, the pomp got beat out of this thing years ago," Eddie said. "Not that I'm judging, I have a deep appreciation for useful junk."

"Don't listen to him," Gregory told the dashboard.

"How are you, anyway?" Eddie asked, eyes carefully on the road. "Feeling okay about getting crowned in a few days?"

"Surprisingly, yes," Gregory said. "Possibly I'm just too tired to sustain any kind of anxiety about it, but I think I'm honestly okay. It'll be a big change, of course, but I've done all I can to be ready."

"You're not worried about the actual event?"

"Oh, no, big state occasions don't bother me. I mostly just repeat what they tell me to repeat. As long as I don't mess up the oath of office or drop the sacred orb of rule, I should be fine."

"The sacred orb of rule?" Eddie asked. "Is that like an actual orb, or is it a kind of metaphorical…" he trailed off when he saw Gregory suppressing a smile. "You lying liar."

"There was, once!" Gregory protested. "I think my grandfather got rid of it. He said it was just an encumbrance."

"A real pain in the orb," Eddie replied. "Can't blame him, though. Change can be a good thing."

"I like to think so. I hope my constituents see it that way," Gregory replied. "I'm not going to make a bunch of policy decisions right up front, but I'm setting up a lot of dominoes for incremental change. You're part of that, actually."

"Me?" Eddie asked, delighted.

"Well, you're keeping it new, aren't you?"

"Doing my best," Eddie agreed.

"There you go. I don't want to drag the country into the modern era; it doesn't need dragging. It's going to be a waltz in that direction. With lots of breaks for snacks," he added. Eddie laughed.

"I like that. A waltz into the future," he said. "I've been thinking about that a lot myself."

"What, modernizing? Photogram isn't new enough for you anymore?"

"Funnily enough, no. There's always another platform on the horizon," Eddie said, watching the landscape pass. "More, I've been thinking about making changes. I'm in a place where I can write my own ticket, which I don't think really came home to me until I just…up and left the country for eight weeks to come here. I have money, I have social clout, I have a network. If I didn't want to do *Truly Tasty* anymore, I wouldn't have to."

"Don't you?"

"Well, I'd like to see it continue, but there's no shortage of people who could take over. I don't mind it, I'm just looking at a lot more possibilities outside of it than I used to have. And the network isn't the one who calls the shots anymore. I could do a new show, or no show at all. I could come out if I wanted."

Gregory glanced at him. "Considering it?"

"Yeah. Making some plans. Nothing I've told my PR team yet, but they knew this was coming eventually."

"I wish you more luck than I had."

"Why, what happened?" Eddie turned to him, brow knitting.

"Nothing specific, just the usual savagery from the tabloids. Dad wasn't thrilled at first but honestly I think mostly because of the press. He's come around since," Gregory added.

"I'll at least hold off until after the coronation – can't be stealing your thunder," Eddie said. "The point of it all is that if I say I'm bisexual or talk about a history of relationships with men, and the network tanks the show or fires me, I don't need them. I don't need *Truly Tasty*."

"What would you do instead?"

"World's my oyster. Could become a personal chef like Simon, but I think I like attention too much," Eddie said ruefully. "Think I mentioned opening some restaurants. I could rest on my laurels. Sell a line of cookware on Photogram. But I've been thinking I'd like to do something less intense. Maybe a traditional cooking show."

"In a studio?" Gregory asked, amused by the visual. "With one of those tastefully cluttered kitchen sets?"

"Studio, maybe, I don't know. Short videos are trendy at the moment and I could do fifteen, twenty shorts in a day. Spend a week on set and stock my Photogram queue for the year. Not that thrilling, though." Eddie sighed. "It's just there's so much food I still don't know how to cook. I'd like to do something where I learn a new dish each week and teach it to the viewers. Eddie Gets Educated."

"Right after Keeping It Noodle, the Rambler tour of Italy," Gregory laughed. "The internet will love it."

They turned onto the main street of town at that point, and Eddie directed him about halfway down, and around to a loading dock on the back. The shop owner, clearly out early specifically to meet Eddie, looked startled to see his king-elect behind the wheel. He bobbed a little bow, took the signed invoice back from Eddie, and vanished into the shop. Gregory, distracted by loading box after box of baskets into the truck, vaguely registered the man handing a solitary basket to Eddie, but didn't think anything of it until they were back on the road.

"Hey, pull over here," Eddie said, after a few minutes of contemplative silence. He gestured to a scenic overlook that gazed down onto the bay and harbor, brilliantly blue in the early morning. Gregory, obedient, pulled the truck into the turnoff and parked it.

"Last Photogram selfie?" he asked, as Eddie got out of the truck.

"No, come on out! I have a surprise for you."

"For me?" Gregory asked, joining Eddie, who was pulling down the tailgate of the truck and perching himself on it comfortably. He had the single basket he'd taken from the shopkeeper carefully cradled in one arm.

"Yeah, c'mere," Eddie said, patting the gate next to him. Gregory slung himself into the space Eddie indicated as Eddie turned to face him. He accepted the basket, perplexed, and lifted the hinged lid, revealing a jaunty blue-and-orange striped fabric lining, in which sat a small paper carton. He lifted the carton out and opened it, torn between confusion and delight. It turned out to be a small cake, about four inches square, covered in white frosting, adorned with blue and orange birds.

"It's a congratulations cake!" Eddie said, excited. "It's for your coronation. Man, that came out great," he added, admiring it.

"Bit small for the feast," Gregory said, but he knew his voice gave away how touched he was.

"Ah, this is all for you. Well, and a little for me," Eddie admitted, taking two forks out of the basket. "It seemed like…I don't know, all this fuss is more for the country than for you. You're going to have to spend the whole time vowing or praying or glad-handing. So this is a cake of your very own. Nothing better than cake for breakfast."

"Thank you, Eddie," Gregory said, accepting one of the forks and taking a corner off neatly. "Lord, that's good," he added, around the first mouthful. It was a chocolate cake with what tasted like pomegranate filling between its two layers, and some kind of extra-rich frosting.

"Yeah, you all make some pretty decent cakes," Eddie said, taking a lump of frosting from the other side. "I'm glad you like it."

"I do. The coronation will be fun, but…well, I suppose in the way being married is fun," Gregory said. "The day is all about the person, of course, the king – I mean I will be the one the cameras are on all day. But everything will happen around me. I'm a bit at the whim of fate at that point."

"Well, now that I know you don't have a sacred orb of rule, I might have to make one out of a water balloon and really liven up the coronation," Eddie said. Gregory laughed, taking another bite of cake.

"You wouldn't really," he said.

"No. I'm irreverent but I'm not mean. Anyway, I won't have the time. Once you sit down, I stand up and start moving."

"Hm." Gregory considered it – all of it, really. The warmth of the truck's tailgate under them, the chocolate and pomegranate, the bright blue of the water below, the shadow of the palace behind them. It was wonderful; it was *comfortable* in a way little in his life ever was. Very tempting, in some ways.

"Who was the best king?" Eddie asked, helping himself to more cake. "Like, in all of the history of the country, which king was the greatest? Who is Askazer-Shivadlakia's King Arthur?"

"Gilles Roman y Askaz," Gregory said promptly. "He was the king who united Shivadlakia and Askaz and made it stick. Tradition says he's actually an ancestor of Alanna's but we've never bothered to verify it."

"I'm picturing Alanna in armor on a horse and I'm not hating the visual," Eddie said.

"I think he did do some conquering in his youth and he was a famous swordsman, but he united the two nations through diplomacy and charm. He married a Shivadh princess."

"Slay a dragon first?" Eddie asked, grinning.

"Sadly for us, no. There's an epic about him on a wolf hunt, but it's declasse at this point, since we like wolves and maintain a conservation program for them." Gregory offered Eddie the rest of the cake, setting his fork aside. "He already had two mistresses – "

"Oho!" Eddie cackled.

"It was a *long time ago*," Gregory retorted. "Anyway, he was out riding the border of Askaz, and oral history tells us he was trying to think of a way to unite the sea-bordered Shivadlakia with his own inland kingdom, because he knew with unfettered access to a harbor his merchants would be unstoppable. He was considering invading when he saw a beautiful woman bow-hunting a deer. She shot the deer but it leapt, and it fell on his side of the border. She shouted at him not to touch it because it was hers, he shouted back it was on his land and that was poaching, and she got so angry she pulled him off his horse and tried to take a swing."

"Love at first sight," Eddie said.

"For him, it was. He supposedly wrote in a letter to someone or other that he knew instantly that she was his…well, the old language isn't precise when it comes to being translated into English, but roughly, he knew she was his soulmate."

Eddie digested this, along with some cake, pondering it. "What happened to the deer?" he asked finally.

"That's what you want to know?"

"Perfectly good venison going to waste. I hope he let her take it or he's no gentleman."

Gregory grinned. "He did. More or less. While she was butchering it he built a fire and offered to cook some, because it meant she'd hang around a little longer while he figured out who she was and how to get her to come meet him again."

"So he cooked his love a meal?" Eddie beamed. "My kind of story, Greg."

"More than you know. There's an apocryphal version that I've always been fond of, which says it was the princess's brother that shot the deer and got into a fight with him over it, and he married her to stay close to him," Gregory said. "It is historically confirmed that the queen's brother was a close advisor to the royal family for their entire reign."

"Close advisor," Eddie said, eyebrows waggling.

"Well, exactly."

"No shit!"

"They're the reason the country has a…relaxed attitude about that kind of thing. At least, that's my theory. I can thank Gilles Roman y Askaz for my stellar reputation despite my many handsome boyfriends," Gregory said, grinning sidelong at him. "I'm surprised you didn't come across at least one version in all your folk research, but it's not a story we tell often to outsiders. Might have to change that when I'm king, maybe commission a play from the national theatre."

"Well, as long as it's in a park, I'll come watch it," Eddie said.

"That'd be nice. But you're leaving soon – we'll have to schedule it for some future visit."

"I could leave soon," Eddie said, looking out over the harbor. "Or I could stay a little while longer."

Gregory tilted his head. "After the banquet, you mean? I assumed you'd have a lot to do, given all your plans."

"Sure. But I could do them all here." Eddie turned to him. "Especially if the network wanted to cancel me, I'd really have no good reason to go back to the US. I'm several hours away from my biggest demographic here, so I could do pretty much what I wanted without having to give a damn about my numbers. I said I wouldn't cheapen your coronation by making it about me, and I meant that, but a week or two after..." he shrugged. "I think...I know what I said a couple of weeks ago and I *know* it's only been a couple of weeks, but I think there's something here worth staying for. Isn't there?"

Gregory knew what he was asking, and it made him lightheaded, but the little anchor deep inside him, the one that was preparing to be king, held him back.

"The problem," he said slowly, "is that it would be...nice, and convenient, and maybe even as good and functional as you think – but it would be a solution to a problem, and I don't want to make you that."

"What, good and functional?" Eddie asked lightly.

"A solution," Gregory said. "You're a person."

"I like solving problems," Eddie pointed out. "I don't mind it."

"I'm worried that would change," Gregory replied. "My life, Eddie – it's not my own. It belongs to the country. Anyone who serves the country has to feel the same, and you've only just finished telling me about how you can finally do just as you like. I wouldn't ruin that for you, not for anything."

Eddie seemed to be considering this, with none of his usual blithe disregard for reality.

"I suppose I see what you mean," he said at last. "And we've had the conversation about...sacrifice."

"So you understand," Gregory said, relieved, because honestly if Eddie had tried to argue...

"I do. Not sure I completely agree, but I understand," he said. "And...at least this way it's settled. Come on, let's get going," he added, hopping down and heading for the door of the truck. "Busy day ahead."

"You're all right, though," Gregory said, a half-question, as he started the truck up again.

"Sure," Eddie replied, his smile sunny and, as far as Gregory could tell, real. "I'm the one who said this could just be fun. And it has been, so no regrets," he added, and kissed Gregory on the cheek before settling back on his side of the truck.

THE CORONATION DAY OF HIS MAJESTY KING GREGORY III

EDDIE, STANDING IN the kitchen in his most comfortable shoes and his tallest chef's hat, clapped his hands for attention. Simon, three sous chefs, and innumerable prep chefs and waiters all looked up from where they were setting up their stations.

"Greetings, patriotic comrades," he announced, and they laughed lightly. "Welcome to zero day. In less than twelve hours we will be feeding the nobility of Askazer-Shivadlakia – "

He waited for the applause over his flawless pronunciation to die down.

" – as well as diplomats, politicians, industrialists, rich fuckwits, and other powerful people from powerful places," he said. "If you have ever brought your A-game, I need it today. Don't think about the time limit or what's going on in the palace, just think about making the absolute best, most impressive food you can make. Nobody is getting fired for screwing up today, so if you do screw up you need to tell me as soon as possible so I can fix it. Is there anyone who does not know what they're doing?"

He held up his own hand, to a sprinkling of laughter.

"Is there anyone who has a question or a problem?"

Silence.

"In that case, get going," Eddie said, clapping Simon on the back. "Battle stations – let's show 'em what we're made of!"

Coronations didn't come around very often, which Gregory supposed was probably for the best. He hadn't been born yet when his father was crowned. He'd been to one or two in other countries during his childhood, but he'd generally been given a toy to play with quietly while his mother and father paid attention to the ceremony. He'd been through portions of his own crowning in rehearsal but not the whole thing at once, and he didn't realize how dull some parts were.

It opened with a reading of the history of the monarchy, which was mostly boring because Gregory already knew it and also they didn't keep any of the interesting trivia in. To keep his mind occupied, he counted fancy hats in the audience and tried to decide which, if any, would be likely to become a meme; then he tried valiantly to put a name to every face he could see, and awarded himself about a 75% success rate. He identified at least one Photogram influencer who had managed somehow to sneak in, but before he could find a way to notify anyone, the sergeant at arms had noticed and quietly taken her phone away. She looked annoyed until Gregory caught her eye and winked at her, which settled her down and made her blush a little.

He returned his attention to the reading just in time for the master of ceremonies to reach the end of the recitation.

"King Michaelis I, son of King Jason I the Interloper," the man intoned, filling the word *interloper* with amused irony. Most of the population, Dad included, thought it was hugely funny that Granddad, the duly elected king, was called an interloper. That's what you got for interrupting a few centuries of hereditary rule, Dad said. "Today, we crown King Gregory III, son of King Michaelis I and Miranda, Queen of Askazer-Shivadlakia, duly elected by ballot of the will of the people of Askazer-Shivadlakia."

First time bowing; Gregory stood, bowed, swooped his robes a little to situate them more comfortably, and sat back again. There was polite applause.

His father, in a special audience alcove where very few other than Gregory could see him, rolled his eyes. It was going to be a long day.

Still, there were moments when Gregory felt a strange spark, a sense of unreality that this was happening. It was almost supernatural. In rehearsal, stuff like kneeling to accept the ceremonial sword, wrapped in a length of fishing-boat hawser, had seemed silly at best. Now there was the hush of a room of witnesses, and the hairs on his arms stood on end as he took the sword.

He did struggle to stay awake during some of the singing, which was operatic and not really his bag. And then, the crown was finally placed on his head…

Well, he was probably just tired, and overwhelmed from the long day. It was just that when he felt it settle over his hair, a crown his father and grandfather and at least a few of his mother's ancestors had worn, he felt like there was a sudden tether in his chest, tying him to his country, rooting him as part of the land. He understood, if only fleetingly, old legends about the king's spiritual communion with the people.

Then the kneeling pages were rising and the master of ceremonies was coming around from crowning him to shake his hand, and people were taking pictures and beginning to stand to process out from the very humid throne room. Gregory stood, waiting by custom until the last of the witnesses had left. Michaelis, second-to-last out, stopped to give him a brief hug and whisper a reassurance in his ear before leaving.

"And now I'm king," Gregory III murmured to himself, before gently shedding the official robe of office on the throne and walking to the doorway, where Alanna was standing with his uniform jacket.

"Good job," she said, helping him into the jacket and smoothing it across his shoulders.

"I do sit *and* bow like an absolute champion," he replied. She beamed.

"Ready to party till dawn?"

"Is that a coffee?" he asked, blindsided as she produced a covered cup from a little table nearby.

"Cold brew, sugar, milk," she said, and he gulped it greedily. "Thought you could use a pick-me-up."

"Thank goodness. Do I have three minutes for the restroom?"

She nodded and took the cup back from him as he dashed across the hall. By the time he emerged, Jerry had joined her. He was wearing a magnificent floor-length orange evening gown with blue trim, and orange opera gloves to match.

"Come on, come on, everyone's in the garden," Jerry said, leading him towards the party. "It looks amazing, Greg. Sire," he added impudently.

"So do you. Out to make every tabloid front page tomorrow morning?" Gregory asked, gesturing at the gown.

"Do you like it? Figured it was about time I did something unexpected, and it takes a little heat off you."

"Thank you. It does suit you," Gregory agreed. "By the way, Alanna says I need to make you my vizier. What did you do to get made vizier?"

"Never you mind. Is there a ceremony?"

"Not that I know of, but I'm sure you can invent one. Make yourself up a robe and some kind of medallion of office while you're at it," Gregory answered, and stepped through the doorway into a kind of warm fantasy world.

The garden had been filled with tables covered with checked tablecloths and a basket on each, just as Eddie had described. Overhead, paper lanterns were hung from wooden poles, waiting to be lit when it was dark out. There were croquet wickets set up at the far end, past the small stage for the musicians and a temporary parquet floor that had been installed for dancing. People were finding their seats, poking curiously at the baskets, and making small talk with one another, enjoying the warm afternoon. A traditional Shivadh folk quartet was tuning up on the stage.

The nearest people noticed Gregory emerge and began to clap; the applause rippled outward, and Gregory smiled deprecatingly and gave a wave, the same wave his father often gave at state events. Jerry subtly broke a path for them as Alanna guided him to the king's table, where Michaelis, Jerry, Jerry's mother, Alanna's grandparents, and a handful of diplomats were seating themselves. The diplomats looked aghast at Jerry, but the nobility didn't even bother batting an eye.

"Crown's crooked," Michaelis said, reaching out to Gregory to straighten it. "There. Can't look disreputable for at least another few hours."

"Thanks," Gregory said distractedly, seating himself. Around them, everyone else took their seats too. There was what felt like an indrawn breath, and then from seeming nowhere an army of waitstaff appeared, thermoses in hand, laying bowls before the assembled guests to serve out the hot soup and cold potato salad. People began to eat hungrily, chattering to each other about the weather, the coronation, the food. Gregory felt he should probably make the speech he'd prepared, but the noise level was rising…

Jerry, catching his eye, stood up and began tapping his spoon against his glass, calling for quiet. Voices settled, and even the clink of spoons in bowls stopped.

"Attention everyone! As your new grand vizier to the king, allow me to introduce to you King Gregory III, who has some notes prepared," he said, bowing at Gregory, who stood and nodded back.

"Thank you, Gerald," he said, which drew a face from Jerry. "I promise to be brief. Gathered dignitaries, friends, allies, and I'm sure one or two spies…"

The crowd laughed on cue, thank goodness.

"I would like to thank you all for attending the coronation today," he said. "I am so pleased and proud to represent the third generation of my family to rule by popular acclaim. I hope I will rule as wisely – and as long – as my father," he added, nodding at Michaelis, who acknowledged it with a wave.

"Ruling a kingdom is an incredibly complex task, and my ministers and staff have been very patient with me," he continued. "Tomorrow we begin a long job of work, maintaining the peace and prosperity the country owes to its people. All I can do is keep a hand on the rudder. I trust you all to tell me if we're steering into rough waters."

He took a breath, because it seemed difficult to catch it. "In the meantime, we are grateful for your ongoing support. I would be remiss not to credit our dear Alanna, who was instrumental in planning all of today; my father, King Emeritus Michaelis – " he paused for applause, and his father looked faintly embarrassed but nodded regally, "– and all of the palace staff, who have been very tolerant of the disruption to our normally quiet life. I hope you also enjoy the wonderful picnic meal, cooked by our very popular and very…boisterous friend, Mr. Eddie Rambler, and our palace chef of many years, Simon LeFevre."

He saw movement out of the corner of his eye; Simon giving a little wave, standing next to Eddie at the edge of the picnic ground, both in chef's whites pristine enough they must have changed for the feast.

"As I expect any member of the palace to do, Alanna and my father, our staff and friends, have also often reminded me of my responsibility to serve the country first, to preserve the best of our traditions, and to maintain a sense of awe at the honor I've been given," he said. "Please enjoy the food, the dancing to come, and the company of one another in this spirit: that today we celebrate not only a coronation but a long tradition of excellence in our small but proud nation."

He sat down amid cheers and applause, and a renewed interest in the food; Michaelis leaned over and said, "A good speech. Glad you kept it short."

"Me too," Gregory replied with a grin. "Thank you, father."

"I do wonder, though," Michaelis said, as he started on the mushroom soup.

"Oh? About what?" Gregory asked.

"Well, your mother and I raised you to serve the country and consider the needs of others, given how fortunate we've been," Michaelis said. "Lessons you took to heart, obviously. And all this talk of duty to country is fine and admirable."

"But?" Gregory asked, curious as to where this was going.

"But I wonder if I forgot to tell you that a king should also be happy," Michaelis said.

"I wouldn't have taken the job if I didn't love it. Of course I'm happy," Gregory assured him. "Starving, but happy."

"Good. Eat up now. People will want to come bend your ear soon enough," Michaelis said. "Gerald!"

"Uncle?" Jerry asked.

"Do your best to keep publicity hounds and that woman who snuck in from the internet away from Gregory for a bit, would you?"

Jerry laughed. "That woman from the internet has more followers than the population of the country, but I'll do my best."

"Make sure she gets her phone back, it can't harm anyone at this point," Gregory added. "Find her somewhere to sit, tell her the king apologizes for the inconvenience, and get her to share any flattering photos she may have managed to take."

Jerry laughed. "On it, boss," he said, and took a glass of wine and a sandwich with him as he wandered off.

"Don't let him give her your phone number, you'll never hear the end of it," Michaelis said.

"I doubt he'll remember past *go talk to the pretty woman from the internet*," Gregory replied. He craned his head around to see if Eddie was still there, but he'd disappeared, probably back into the kitchen with

Simon. Michaelis followed his gaze.

"The staff will look after themselves," his father said. "And they have outdone themselves on this soup, so let's not make their work meaningless by letting it get cold."

Gregory smiled and bent to his dinner. "Right you are, Dad."

Eddie set up the camera on a tiny portable tripod, perched gently on a sculpted topiary bush with a flat top. He checked the stability and then the angle, adjusting it so that the just-lit lanterns and a small sliver of the party was visible behind him. Finally, he pressed the record button, pulling his hat off.

"I don't mind telling everyone, I am worn out," he said, giving them a wide grin to show it was a good tired. "Everything went off without a hitch, though — or at least with only the normal number of hitches. I know you all come here for the real talk that I don't always have time for on *Truly Tasty*, so this is your semi-annual reminder that screwups in a kitchen are normal, and the mark of a good chef is in how you handle the unexpected. But today we had very few!"

He held up a hand, gesturing to the party going on behind him. "For all my followers in-country, congratulations on your new king! He did great today and I'm sure he'll rule wisely. They're partying until dawn and so should you. For the rest of my followers, it's like mid-morning where most of you are, I think? Maybe don't start drinking until you get off work. I was gonna go grab a cocktail myself, but I think I'm ready for bed. My work here is done, honestly. All except the dishes, anyway, and someone else is being paid to wash those."

He laughed, mopping his forehead with the edge of his hat.

"I was thinking about staying a few extra days but I traveled light coming here, so it's easy enough to pick up and go — you know me, I always have places to go, stuff to do, new food to eat. So tomorrow morning I'll probably be off on a new adventure!"

Behind him, the music struck up, which he took as a cue to wrap — his followers didn't like music or other noise under his videos, generally, unless it was kitchen noises.

"You all got a great place here," he said. "I know my motto's always been about keeping it new, but there's something to be said for age – newness is about reinvention, reimagination, not necessarily never getting to touch any history. You can't change something if you don't understand it, after all. Anyway, I'm gonna miss this place. Might make it back here someday soon though! I'd like to do a show that brings people a real taste of the region. Next time you see me I might be on a train, or in Paris, or maybe back in Messina – but for now this is Eddie Rambler, reminding you to keep it new, and signing off."

He stopped the recording, taking his phone off the tripod and settling onto a decorative bench that was probably older than America, and definitely older than he was, to do a few minor edits. There was the sound of a throat clearing, and he looked up, startled.

"I didn't want to interrupt your recording," King Michaelis – ex-king? Was it really King Emeritus? He should have looked up what you call a former king – stood nearby, hands in the pockets of his sober black uniform.

"Your Retired Majesty," Eddie said. "Give me thirty seconds and I'll check with the internet what I'm supposed to call you."

Michaelis gave him a tired smile. "Technically still Your Majesty, but that will become confusing, I suspect. For direct address, I find 'Your Grace' rarely goes amiss. Vague enough not to break protocol, strange enough it's probably an honor to be called it."

"Well, Your Grace, what can I do for you? Sneaking off for a smoke?" Eddie asked, feeling a little daring.

"I was coming to find you, actually," he said.

"Oh, no – is something wrong – "

"No, nothing to worry about," Michaelis said quickly. "It's a great success, in fact. Many, many drunk people."

Eddie smiled. "How's the king?"

"He's holding up. I wanted to speak to you about him, actually. May I sit?"

"It's your bench, technically," Eddie said, gesturing to the other half of it, turning to face him as the former king settled himself. Michaelis held his hands between his knees, leaning forward, seemingly in thought.

"I'm not sure, when Gregory was born, that we wanted him to be king," he said slowly. "His mother was ambivalent about the nobility, having come from it, and we both knew by then that it could be stressful. Difficult. You've seen, I think, what Gregory's been up to since you arrived."

"Seems like a lot of work, but he likes it," Eddie ventured.

"He does, thank goodness. I think the only reason I trust it's his choice is that he so clearly saw how conflicted we were over the idea. He'll be a good king as long as he keeps his wits about him." Michaelis inhaled, let out the breath, then breathed in to speak again. "I made an error with him, though. I think I made him think that it was all or nothing, that service to the crown meant one couldn't have things for oneself. I thought he'd see that he and his mother were precious to me for reasons having nothing to do with her being the queen or him being my heir. But before the coronation – a few months ago – I told him he needed to find a partner. It's an important role in our government, the…well, traditionally the queen, but that's a loaded word when one's son prefers men."

Eddie couldn't help himself; he snickered. Michaelis glanced at him and nodded.

"Just so," he agreed. "Perhaps I put too much pressure on him. And perhaps the affair you've been having with my son really is just a last fling before he takes on all this responsibility."

That dropped the smile off Eddie's face. "We didn't know you knew."

"I didn't rule a country for decades by being unobservant," Michaelis replied. "I'm not angry. Even if I were, what would I do about it? You're both grown men. I'm just telling you I know, and also that if…if it is more, then you, and I, and Gregory all have a significant problem."

Eddie tilted his head. "Which is?"

"He clearly thinks he needs to marry someone appropriate. Someone of the blood, or at the least someone who can help him rule. Perhaps he thinks that isn't you, and perhaps it isn't, but…"

"Ah," Eddie said. Michaelis gave him a curious look. "That's not it, but you're close."

"Do tell."

"He said I was a solution to a problem," Eddie said. Michaelis nodded. "But he also said I was a person, and he wasn't going to treat me like I wasn't."

"Well." Michaelis considered this. "That is both the smartest and stupidest thing he's said since the puffin incident."

"The…puffin…?"

"I'll let him tell you that one – or better yet, ask Alanna," Michaelis said. "I suppose what I'd like to know is…are you? Or could you be?"

"A solution?" Eddie shrugged. "Who knows? I like him. I like him enough I asked to stay, and I respect him enough that when he said no, I agreed. Do I think it would be weird and cool to be – " he grinned at Michaelis, " – *queen* of a country? Sure. It's soon to know exactly how I feel about your son, but I love this place. I could see a life here. But it's all still new and shiny to me, and he's smart not to ask on those terms."

"But on other terms, you might stay. Just to see," Michaelis said slowly.

"I'd have to wrap up some business in America and I don't know how good your spies are, but I'm about to very publicly come out as bisexual, which could draw attention Greg doesn't want if I do stay. But sure, if I had a reason that wasn't about the king, I wouldn't mind."

Michaelis nodded. "When were you planning to go?"

"Tomorrow, early."

"Ah. There's a little more broken heart there than evident?"

Eddie blinked at him. "Yeah, maybe."

"Well, before you go, speak to Alanna," Michaelis said. "She may have some final business for you."

Eddie nodded, puzzled and confused but also well aware that something momentous was happening. "Thank you. I'll do that."

Michaelis nodded and stood, dusting down his trousers. "Goodnight, Chef."

"Goodnight, Your Grace."

Michaelis snorted, heading back towards the party, and Eddie sat on the bench for a good five minutes, trying to work out what exactly had just happened, before he came to his senses. He looked down at his phone, pushed the post button on Photogram to send the video he'd filmed before the king arrived, and then stood up, stretching, and went to bed.

FIRST DAY OF
THE REIGN OF HIS MAJESTY
KING GREGORY III

GREGORY HAD GIVEN the staff the day off after the coronation, which was the only rational thing to do. Most of them had worked for days leading up to the coronation and some had worked until dawn the night before, serving at the party. Giving the administrative staff the day off meant they could give most of the kitchen staff the day off as well.

He'd told Simon he should take the day, but he doubted Simon had listened, and the smell from the kitchen told him he was right. He popped his head in to find Simon making crepes at the stove.

"Good morning, Sire," Simon said with a small grin.

"I'm going to have to get used to that. Morning," Gregory yawned, already missing Eddie's noisy presence in the kitchen most mornings. Better this way, but...he'd probably feel the absence for a while.

"There are crepes also in the dining room, and fillings to put into them. Leftovers from last night, mostly, but I've cooked the last of the fruit in a sugar syrup, there are mushrooms sauteed with shallots, and the potato salad is always better the second day, you know."

"Surprised there's any left."

"A very popular dish," Simon agreed. "Any requests?"

Privately he wondered if there were any chicken wings available, but that was just silly nostalgia.

"No, I'll browse the dining room," he said. "Coffee?"

"In the carafe."

"Dad?"

"Awake and scheming. Being king always kept him out of trouble," Simon observed.

"I'll do my best to find him a hobby," Gregory replied. "I'll be in the dining room if anyone comes looking."

Simon acknowledged him with a wave as he left, sleepily ambling his way to the dining room. When he was about ten feet away he heard Alanna's voice, slightly raised, vigorously defending…thick-cut bacon?

" – supposed to have texture," she was saying, her voice strident. "You're supposed to really experience it."

"Flavor is an experience," said another voice, and Gregory stopped, startled. "When you slice it thinly, the fat renders out – "

"Exactly! The fat's supposed to be there!" Alanna argued.

Gregory hurried forward and then stopped again in the doorway, perplexed by the scene in front of him.

Michaelis was sitting at the dining table as usual, quietly eating a crepe stuffed with fruit, a little bowl of oatmeal at his elbow. Alanna was sitting near him, tablet discarded on the table, hands gesturing as she vigorously defended traditional Askazer bacon, which had more in common with pork belly than American breakfast meat. She was turned slightly so that she faced…

Eddie, who was sitting next to her and apparently arguing with her for the benefit of his camera, which was filming the whole thing from the far side of the table.

Eddie's back was to him and blocking Alanna's line of sight to the doorway, but Michaelis had a clear view and noticed Gregory immediately.

"Sire," he drawled.

Alanna's head shot up in surprise; Eddie turned, but not to Gregory. Instead he reached out and ended the camera recording before twisting around.

"Eddie," Gregory said, realizing how obvious he sounded even as he said it.

"Way to interrupt filming, Your Majesty," Eddie replied. "That was great though," he added to Alanna. "We can continue discussing how wrong you are later."

"I'm not wrong!" Alanna insisted.

"She has strong feelings about pork," Eddie told Gregory.

"Better her than me, I guess, I don't eat it," Gregory said. "What are you doing here?"

"Eatin' breakfast," Eddie said. "Starting trouble. The usual."

"He's good at both," Michaelis put in.

"I thought you were leaving," Gregory said.

Eddie chuckled. "Saw my video, huh?"

Gregory held up his phone. "Photogram sends me a little notice when you post."

"Plans changed," Eddie said. "Just waiting for my PR guys back in the states to wake up before I run this up their flagpole, but engagement's been off the charts since I got here and Alanna says once they fixed the tourism website they started getting tons of interest. In the next six months they expect tourism's gonna double – overseas tourism might even triple."

"…and?" Gregory asked, bewildered, finally coming into the room to sit down. Michaelis pushed a bowl of potato salad towards him gently.

"And that means that the communications team needs some help," Alanna said. "We're hiring Eddie."

"I'm going to make a bunch of videos on like…local culture," Eddie said. "You know, where to get the best coffee, how to talk to the locals, the best way to get the train here from Paris, that kind of thing. Where to rent bicycles and where to ride them. Oh! And how the surfing is. Excited to try that."

"I thought you were going to start a cooking show," Gregory replied.

"I could, but I can do that anywhere I've got a clean corner of a kitchen to cook in," Eddie said. "I can cook here as well as anywhere."

"Here, in Askazer-Shivadlakia?"

"Well, I finally learned how to pronounce it," Eddie said, as Simon came in with a fresh plate of crepes. "You'll help, Simon, won't you?"

"I'd like a raise," Simon told Gregory.

"Probably due," Gregory agreed, turning back to Eddie.

"Anyway I need to file a bunch of tax stuff, but there was no reason not to get started immediately, so I asked Alanna for her thoughts and she said Americans do bacon wrong, which is a hill I was surprised to find I would die on," Eddie said.

"Keep eating Askazer bacon and you probably will," Gregory replied, deciding that whatever was going on, it was probably best to just lean in. He spooned some potato salad into a crepe and took a bite. Eddie turned to Alanna and gestured at Gregory as if to say, *See? The king agrees with me.*

"Oh, like I've never told him to his face he's wrong and stupid before," Alanna sniffed. "Sire, I'm going to hire this man but I'd like it recorded that he's wrong about bacon."

"Keep me out of it," Gregory said. "He's your problem now."

"I strongly doubt that," Michaelis murmured, and Gregory and Alanna both looked at him in surprise. Eddie seemed smug. Michaelis, finishing his oatmeal, stood and set his napkin aside, bending to rest a hand on Gregory's shoulder.

"Be happy, sire," he said, turning to leave. "And good luck!" he called from the hallway.

"Does he….?" Gregory pointed after his father, but he was looking at Eddie.

"Apparently we've been 'obvious'," Eddie said, employing airquotes. Then, possibly just to annoy him, he added, "And he thinks a good 'work life balance' is 'important'."

"So I'm coming to understand," Gregory admitted.

"Look, nothing's set in stone," Eddie said. "But it wouldn't be awful if we decided to consider the possibility. I'm extremely charming and functional once you get to know me."

"Sure, that's what they all say," Gregory replied.

"Your dad seems to have pulled a u-turn on me from where he was a few weeks ago, anyhow," Eddie offered.

"He has very strong opinions."

"Yeah, that definitely doesn't run in the family," Alanna put in, gathering up her tablet. "I'm going to tactfully withdraw and let you two figure this out," she announced. "I'll have your nine o'clock briefing ready, Greg, but I can tell you it's going to be a blank page because anyone who didn't take the day is hungover or still drunk."

"Good, I suspect I'll need some time," Gregory replied, not looking away from Eddie as Alanna left. They were quiet for a few seconds, Eddie patiently waiting for something, Gregory sorting his thoughts.

"You understand," he said slowly, "you will need a royal visa to remain in-country and work for the palace. The normal visas generally take several weeks and if you want to make official content for royal communications, we'll have to fast-track that."

"Well, I know a guy," Eddie pointed out.

"And if you hold a royal exception visa, you represent the royal family," Gregory continued thoughtfully. "That's a heavy responsibility, Eddie. I'd want to personally teach you what you needed to know. And everyone here knows everything about the royal family, so our attentions towards you won't go unremarked."

"I think I'll survive," Eddie said quietly.

"If you, say, wanted to have dinner with me. Or go bowfishing at the lodge. People might talk."

"I'm ready to let 'em if you are," Eddie said.

"Yes. I suppose I am, actually," Gregory replied. Eddie reached out and tugged Gregory's wrist, pulling him out of his seat and into Eddie's lap, which was undignified, but also felt right. The way the coronation had. Like a puzzle piece settling into place, or a tether being tied.

"I have an idea for a coming-out video but it's gonna require multiple filming locations and some special effects," Eddie said, his face serious. "There may be some extremely tacky choreography. I can't promise good taste."

"Why start now?" Gregory asked, and Eddie cracked up laughing. Gregory leaned down to kiss him, fingers threading through Eddie's wild hair, eventually settling in the bright pink collar of his loud flower-print shirt.

EPILOGUE

EDDIE CHECKED HIS tie and waistcoat one final time, turned to his king, and said, "Tasty?"

Gregory, adjusting his collar in the mirror, rolled his eyes and nodded. Eddie shot him a grin.

"I'm in very nice black evening wear," Eddie said, wrapping his arms around Gregory from behind. Gregory took the opportunity to fix Eddie's cufflinks. "The flower pattern on the waistcoat is extremely traditional, the tailor said so."

"After you asked him what the loudest possible print you could get away with was," Gregory pointed out.

"You love it."

"I am, in fact, extremely fond of your loudness," Gregory agreed. "It's a real failure of character on my part, everyone says so."

Eddie kissed his neck and released him, hopping up to sit on the low table in the dressing room. "You ready for tonight?"

"Sure. What's not to enjoy? It's the one year anniversary of the coronation, the party will be mellow, and you'll be there."

"As your boyfriend for the first time."

"Nonsense," Gregory said. "Everyone knows we've been dating. You've been at every state event I could drag you to. This is just a formality, introducing you as a companion to the king. I'd have done it sooner if you asked."

"No reason to. Like you said, everyone knew. Nice to make it official, though," Eddie said, beaming. "And I have to say, I love all the fuss. I have never met anyone who likes drama as much as the whole population of Askazer-Shivadlakia."

"It's not drama, it's pageantry."

"I'm sure they love drama too. Bet you if we staged a fight, the entire country would be up in arms. You could start a civil war."

"The country was united centuries ago. If I tear it apart because I had a fight with my boyfriend, I'll never live it down," Gregory told him. "Now, you remember about the processional?"

Eddie nodded. "It's not like I haven't seen one before. You're called and you process into the ballroom, then your father and the family, then heads of Parliament. The royal dates come after. Fun to be with them instead of waiting for you to arrive this time."

"But you'll be first, so you'll need to listen sharp for your name."

"Mr. Eddie Rambler!" Eddie boomed.

"Well, Edward, but yes," Gregory said. There was a strangely tense pause. "Eddie?"

"When I gave the announcer the little card with my name, I wrote Eddie on it," Eddie said. "Is that okay?"

"It's a formal announcement. They'll use your legal name regardless of what's on the card."

Eddie frowned. "But they'll just assume it's Edward, right?"

"Generally they make a note when they do the background check, but in your case they probably just looked up your pay stub from…" Gregory trailed off, because Eddie's eyes kept getting bigger. "Your legal name *is* Edward Rambler, isn't it?"

"Uh, the Rambler part's right," Eddie said.

"Your name's not Edward?" Gregory asked. "We've been dating for a year. Simon told me your name was Edward. My father's been calling you Edward."

"Look, it's not that I don't like my name," Eddie said. "Or that I have a criminal past or something. Well, I do, but not like that. I just never think about it until it's already awkward."

"Eddie, what on Earth is your name?" Gregory demanded, in his best royal tone.

"In my defense, it's easier than Askazer-Shivadlakia," Eddie said.

"Mr. Theophile Rambler and Lady Alanna Daskaz!" a voice called, and Eddie did his best to proceed forward with dignity.

Technically, Alanna should have gone into the ballroom with the royal cousins, following Gregory. She was high enough born, and she was very evidently one of the King's favorite people. But tonight she was on the arm of a visiting diplomat who was going in with the heads of Parliament, so she was relegated to the Very Important Dates part of the processional.

"I cannot believe your name is Theophile," she said, as she and Eddie descended the stairs to the ballroom. "How did you get Eddie from Theophile?"

"My parents are hippies with real weird theology," Eddie said around a smile for the cameras. "Everyone called me Ted but one of my brothers couldn't say his Ts, so everyone started calling me Ed. Eddie is just more TV-friendly."

"I would have given you so much endless flak for being named Theophile, but that's actually very sweet so now I can't," Alanna said.

"You are reacting way more maturely than Gregory," Eddie told her, handing her off to her adoring diplomat and making his way to the king's side, in the line to receive their guests.

"I don't even know who you are," Gregory said, eyes still forward as Eddie joined him.

"That's not what you said last night," Eddie answered. Gregory's lips twitched.

"Where were you last night? Because I was in bed with some guy named Theophile."

"Alanna thinks it's a very nice name," Eddie said.

"When we were both six I watched Alanna eat a ladybug," Gregory replied.

"Insect protein is the food of the future."

"Sweet nothings," Gregory sighed, as the procession ended. There was a blast of fanfare, and a string quartet struck up what Eddie had come to categorize as Royal Family Muzak: light enough that it didn't interrupt conversation, constant enough to be pleasant background noise. Later there would be waltzing, which in this particular royal family always sounded like a threat. Eddie was looking forward to it; this was his first official outing as Gregory's date, where before he'd always attended these things as a guest of the palace.

Usually he took the first dance with Gregory, had a few interesting conversations, and then slipped away while Gregory still had two or three hours of politics ahead of him. It wasn't that he especially minded the politics, but he didn't want to be a distraction, and he liked to take a stroll on the grounds and listen to the party from a distance before heading to bed. Tonight, however, something a little different was on the menu.

"I should demand a traditional Shivadh name," he said to Gregory, as a line formed for people to greet the king.

"So good to see you," Gregory said to a visiting Italian dignitary of some kind, and then to Eddie, "I don't even have a traditional Shivadh name. They tend to be quite complicated."

"Welcome! Man, that jacket looks great on you," Eddie said to the Italian, who beamed at him. "I bet I could rock a Shivadh name. Can't be more obnoxious to say than Theophile."

"Beloved Theophile, I am begging you to focus," Gregory said, and Eddie shot him a grin before composing himself to be as proper as he knew how to be.

Alanna found Jerry hiding in a corner with a cocktail, which was impressive considering they were only serving wine at the ball. She raised an eyebrow at it; he looked unrepentant and offered her a sip.

"No, I'm still on the clock," she told him, leaning against the wall next to him, watching the reception line as the last of the visitors met the king. "Squiring the diplomat and keeping an eye on Gregory for signs of panic."

"As if Greg ever panics at these things. Don't know how he does it."

"I think he likes it. Normally you do too," she pointed out. "Why are you pretending you're not hiding behind a decorative ficus?"

"Do you remember the girl I dated my last year in boarding school?" he asked.

"I remember the grievous bodily harm she threatened you with."

"She's here with her successful husband and their adorable young child and I'm pretending to be petty about it," he said.

"Pretending," she replied skeptically.

"I thought it would make her feel good, and also it means if she still wants to kill me she can't get close enough," he said.

"Well, it's one way to live," she replied. She watched as Gregory, his duties done, took a few steps back and signaled the string quartet to strike up dancing music.

"Theophile looks thrilled to be doing the most boring job on the planet," Jerry said.

"I can't believe that's his name." Alanna shook her head.

"I can, he looks like a Theophile. I've always thought so," Jerry said, mock-serious. Alanna thumped him on the arm.

"Be nice. It's about to be a rollercoaster of an evening," she said.

"What? Why? Did you invite my ex to come say hello?"

"Just wait for it," Alanna told him.

"Still mad at me?" Eddie asked, as he and Gregory took the floor for the first waltz. He was happy to take the formal black gloves off, but after shaking a million hands in the reception line, he was prepared to admit he understood why the royal uniform included them.

"I'm not mad," Gregory told him, sliding an arm around his waist. "This is actually very funny. You'll find out why in about two minutes."

"What happens in two minutes?" Eddie asked. "Do they call my name again for some reason?"

"No," Gregory said, as the music began. "Don't worry about it."

"You're lucky I'm extremely laid back and actually won't," Eddie said.

"I do think I've had good luck," Gregory told him. "I didn't expect you'd tolerate this end of the business so well, Eddie."

"What, the parties? Love a party, you know me."

"I'm only saying, it's difficult to truly know what you're signing on for, dating the king," Gregory said. "I didn't think you really knew what a relationship with me would mean."

"Oh, I absolutely didn't, the last year has been buck wild," Eddie said. "I love both you and this country, but I had no idea what I was getting into."

"You don't regret it, I hope."

"Not for a second," Eddie told him.

"I have to admit, I didn't think you'd be willing to stay in Askazer-Shivadlakia for months on end, let alone consider a life here."

Eddie gave him a warm grin. "Listen, I love America too, but it can't offer me socialized healthcare, let alone a Mediterranean paradise with the king at my feet."

Gregory nodded, seemingly lost in thought for a moment as they danced, and Eddie sobered.

"This is my home now," he said, more earnestly. "I'm on a permanent visa, I'm running a business here…it's not where I thought this job would take me, but my life is here. Hopefully, with you."

Gregory nodded, and then stopped moving. Eddie, surprised, stopped also. So did the music. Everything was suddenly very, very quiet, and all eyes were on them.

Gregory put his hands in the pockets of his dress trousers, then removed them as fists, offering them to Eddie like a grandparent with a piece of candy, making a kid guess which hand it was in. Behind them, someone gasped.

"Greg, what's going on?" Eddie asked in a low voice. Gregory just nodded at his hands. Eddie, perplexed, tapped his left hand.

Gregory turned his hand over, opening it to show his palm. There was a thin silver ring resting in it.

"This is how we propose in Askazer-Shivadlakia," Gregory said. Eddie stared down at the ring. "You got the ring first try, good job."

"Oh snap," Eddie said. Gregory's face took on a faintly put-upon expression.

"Say yes, dumbass!" someone hissed. It sounded like Jerry.

"See, I can't," Eddie said, and Gregory turned pale. Eddie patted his own pockets madly. He'd put it in one of them –

He came up with the little bag out of his waistcoat pocket and hastily dumped the contents into his hand. He hadn't intended to be so public, so he'd just gone with a gag ring, with a giant plastic "diamond" full of glitter in the top. He offered it to Gregory, who stared at it in shock.

"Good timing, bud, I was going to propose in about an hour," Eddie said, and Gregory burst out laughing.

"You absolutely ludicrous clown of a human being," Gregory said, taking the joke ring out of Eddie's fingers and dropping the slim, elegant silver band into Eddie's palm. "I'm dating a cartoon. It's come to this."

"Technically," Eddie said, staggering from Alanna's hug as he put his ring on, "You're *marrying* a cartoon. I'm as surprised as anyone."

"Did you know?" Gregory asked Alanna, who giggled. "She knew I was proposing to you," he said to Eddie. "You knew," he accused, turning back to her, "and you let him think he was going to propose to me, and – "

"She helped me pick out the ring," Eddie confirmed. "We had to mail-order it. Nobody makes a ring ugly enough around here."

"In front of my entire family and half of Parliament," Gregory said, wiping the tears of laughter from the corners of his eyes.

"I was going to be subtle about it," Eddie protested. "You're the one putting on the dog and pony show! Ah – wait!" he cried, pulling his phone out of his back pocket. "Photogram!"

Gregory started laughing again, but he held out his hand so Eddie could get both hands in the picture. The rest of the party crowded around to congratulate them, or got in line for celebratory champagne.

Eddie spoke aloud as he typed the caption for his Photogram. "*Someone get me the name of a good wedding caterer.* Hashtag *shivadh-life*, hashtag *marriage.* Oh shit," he added suddenly, looking up at Gregory. "Did you throw this whole-ass ball just to propose?"

"Well, it was convenient," Gregory said, twisting the ring around on his finger. "I know it's relatively soon, Eddie, but – "

"Hey, I had the same speech written, how 'bout that," Eddie told him, gently cutting him off. "When you know, you know."

Gregory kissed him, carefully decorous for the cameras, and then turned to Alanna.

"Guess what you get," he said, and she stopped laughing abruptly.

"What?" she asked warily.

"You get to plan the wedding," he told her.